DEATH IN THE DRY RIVER

LISA ALLEN-AGOSTINI

Death in the Dry River

Copyright © 2023 by Lisa Allen-Agostini

For further information, please contact:
1000 Volt Press
info@1000voltpress.com

Cover design and book layout: keifel a. agostini.
Find him at keifelagostini.com.

First Edition
ISBN: 978-1-7347422-9-9

For Ishara and Najja, the best stories I ever wrote

CHAPTER ONE

He opened his eyes to see his hands in his lap covered in blood.

Jerking awake, Sonny Stone shot up out of his bentwood rocker to his bare feet. The pool of blood remained on the polished mahogany seat. Not blood, but sunlight sliding through the one pane of red glass above his back window. The sun, high in the mid-afternoon sky, had hit the pane and pushed Sonny into a nightmare.

Or out of one.

Then he recognized a thumping sound.

The boys in the yard behind his one-roomed apartment were playing rounders and his wooden wall was home base.

Thump.

It was accompanied by a rattle this time, the glass shaking slightly in its leading at the force of a small body crashing into the wall beneath it.

Still standing in his dirty white merino and patched khaki pants, Sonny steupsed.

"If allyuh break my glass they go have to call police for me today, you know," he said, loud enough to be heard by the boys outside.

They giggled. Sonny raised his voice to a shout. "Ah say, if allyuh break my glass—"

The threat was interrupted by the crash of breaking glass. A battered cork ball, slowed by its collision with the dimpled clear pane beside the red glass, fell to the floor of Sonny's room. It made a gentle bump when it landed on the dull pine floor.

"Little hooligans!" He spun around, thrust his feet into the woolen alpagats by the single door, and prepared to turn the brass handle. A shard of glass glittered on his left instep. Slowing, he took off the woven sandals one at a time and shook them out carefully before putting them on again.

When the door swung open the boys were gone. Sonny peered down the street just in time to see the last narrow figure fleeing around the corner of George Street. Slamming the door shut behind him he pelted after the boy.

"Little bastard. You feel you getting away but your mother never make enough money in she whole life to buy that window," Sonny muttered under his breath as he ran, long legs pumping.

Someone standing on Duke Street that April day in 1932 would have seen a tall black man in khaki pants and a white cotton vest, his feet in red alpagats, running like the wind behind three little black boys. The two fastest boys peeled away into a yard at the corner of George and Prince Streets, but one, the biggest, kept going. Moving as fast as his knobby knees would churn, the walnut-shell-brown boy took a hard right onto Prince and ran for his life.

Sonny was hardly winded. Running, his reflexes took over. He was fifteen again and felt the whips of cocoa branches on his face as he ran down a hill in Grande Riviere, his bulging calves scraped by weeds and his slender toes squelching in the muck of rotting leaves and flowers on the ground.

The boy kept running, skidding in a puddle when his foot slipped into the murky drain beside the cobbled pavement. He scrambled up, never quite stopping, and took off again.

This was not Grande Riviere but Port of Spain. The smell Sonny inhaled when he ran past the puddle wasn't the dark, sweet velvet of the bush but the sharp and acrid smell of rubbish, stagnant water and piss.

They were close to the river.

The Dry River was a wide, flat, paved canal through which a trickle of water flowed. Its source was the St Ann's River in the lush hills north of the city. During the dry season it devolved into a sullen creek making its way to the Gulf of Paria. Paved only a year earlier, the river's worst excesses of filth were behind it but Sonny still groaned when he realized the little boy he pursued was heading for the track that would take him into the waterway.

"Don't dare jump down in that river, boy!" he shouted, knowing even as he did that the boy planned just that. The woolly head disappeared over the bank.

Sonny slowed to a halt, his feet pounding in the dusty brown grass that lined the bank.

Peering down, he saw the track, a stony, steep path worn into the side of the river by little boys like the one he was chasing. The track ended about five feet above the riverbed, where it gave way to a wall. The boy was nearly gone now.

Sonny was on the verge of turning back when he heard a short, high shriek.

Little boys, when they're frightened, sound just like little girls. All their incipient manhood blows away like mango flowers in a storm leaving only a child and his fear.

Sonny spotted the boy's dingy red and white striped jersey. The boy had come to a stop about thirty yards away and was cringing against the high wall of the river.

"What happen?" Sonny called, instantly forgetting his broken window and his promises of vengeance. "You see a snake? Is all right," Sonny shouted, gingerly going down the crumbling path in the bank, leaving a trail of rolling stones behind his red alpagats as he jumped down. "If you leave it, it wouldn't do you nothing…"

The boy only whimpered.

Sonny trotted past the piles of rotting rubbish through which the stubborn trickle of the river ran. A bloated dead cat, grey fur bristling in the wind, eyes closed to slits; a bag of blackened tomatoes; a soggy, brown leather loafer with no sole; an old paper kite, half its bright yellow life gone; a broken Cockspur Gold bottle, long emptied of rum.

The boy was standing a few feet from a high hump of garbage that looked like a rag picker's bag. Only it wasn't a bag. What looked like rags was a fine sharkskin suit. On a man who lay facedown in the river in a pool of drying blood.

Sonny grabbed the boy and pressed the small, weeping face into his rock-hard belly. The slender shoulders shook.

"Is all right boy. He ain't go do you nothing. Is all right."

They stood there in the hot, fiercely white sun, the boy crying and Sonny thinking. Somebody would have to run to Besson Street to get the inspector, he was thinking. Somebody would have to tell this man's wife or girlfriend or mother that he had met his end in a fine grey sharkskin suit in the Dry River.

The body's already swelling hands were sprawled at its sides and Sonny saw with some surprise that one still grasped the neck of a guitar. The guitar itself was black as ebony and shiny, clearly expensive and well taken care of—until somebody had bashed in its back and snapped the fretboard. The broken body of the guitar was a foot away, tethered to the neck by six thin strings.

The hand on the neck was the color of good cocoa and wore a gold ring, set with a peanut-sized ruby, on the pinkie. The corpse had naturally curly hair, still slick with pomade. Small stones and bits of gravel surrounded the body.

"Come, boy. Come."

Sonny led the boy away, back to the track. Already his small, light-brown face was puffy. Tears had made tracks in the ashy dirt on his cheeks. He had fine, curly hair, growing out of a low haircut. Sonny ruffled it before hoisting the light frame up to the track and pulling himself up behind him. Though the boy's clothes were old and stained—and his black wool short pants were so tight he couldn't close the top two buttons— they were a cut above Sonny's clothes. Expensive, he could tell, by the quality of the weave of the jersey, and the sturdy stitching of the pants. Yet the boy was barefoot and looked like he needed another meal a day, at least. His collarbones were sharp and his high cheekbones gave him a gaunt appearance. His thighs were leanly muscled and his calves nearly non-existent.

"What is your name, boy?"

"Clarence, sir."

His voice, still girlish in his grief, hitched over the last word.

"Where you living?"

"By you, sir."

"What?"

13

"Me and my mother now move in by you, sir. We in the second room in the back."

"And where your mother now, Clarence? Where she working?"

"She does work there, sir. She does wash for white people." Sonny grunted. He held the boy's shoulder lightly as they trudged back to Duke Street. Just before they passed Duncan Street, Sonny spotted another urchin. "Boy! Boy, you want to make a penny?"

The urchin, wearing a threadbare shirt and torn pants, nodded warily.

"Go by Besson Street station and tell Inspector McLeod that it have something in the Dry River he would want to see. Something human."

The urchin's eyes widened and he nodded. Without another word Sonny started walking away.

"Where my penny?"

This boy, only eight at the most, feeling man enough to challenge me, Sonny thought. What happened to the days when children did as they were told?

"Wait by the river, by the Piccadilly bend, and I go come back and give you."

The urchin walked away, breaking into a trot. He stopped and turned around.

"Who to tell him?"

"What?" Sonny asked.

"Who to tell him send the message? He ain't go come unless he know who send the message, sir."

"Tell him Constable Stone. Tell him Constable Johnson Stone."

CHAPTER TWO

The tall, black policeman in shabby home clothes and the slender brown-skinned boy, similarly dressed, walked through the mid-afternoon sunshine in silence. A casual observer may have thought them on an afternoon errand together, a boy and his uncle, perhaps, on a walk to the drug store or the shop, or the bakery, maybe. But a casual observer would have missed the man's grim expression, the boy's wounded gaze.

Port of Spain's cobbled pavements were busy but not crowded. Sharply dressed men, fedoras atilt on slicked back hair, stepped aside for the man to pass with the boy. Women in flour bag dresses, on their way home from the morning shift, eyed the man, slyly hopeful. He was that kind of man.

Johnson Stone, Jr was tall, just over six foot two, and built like a wall, if a wall could look like it was made of molasses. His skin was that black, that shiny. His erect bearing pointed to his nine years as a policeman, but the force hadn't managed to entirely straighten out his cocksure swagger. It was there, somewhere in the music of his lean-hipped stride. His shoulders were broad and muscular, like a stevedore's, and tapered to a trim waist and hard hips. His thighs and calves were straight and as muscular as his shoulders. Long, narrow hands and feet were the only thing on him that could be thought of as less than perfectly masculine. Those, if one got close enough to consider them, were almost pretty.

Though it was the middle of the week, he was out of work clothes. Sonny, as his mother used to call him, was on indefinite suspension. Insubordination, his superiors said. It was a label Sonny would have argued against, had he been given a chance; as it was, he hadn't. He'd been sent home six months before with full pay. Once a month he got back into his crisp black short pants and grey shirt, spit-shined black shoes and white Hardee hat. Once a month he reported to the barracks to see his bosses. Once a month they asked him if he regretted his actions and was ready to reconsider his position. Once a month he said no. It was no surprise they kept sending him back home.

He passed most of the time of day in his little room, its dark stained pine floors dull with age and lack of attention. The only shining wood in the whole place was the bentwood rocker that was polished by his bottom in the khaki pants he wore every day.

The room was hardly furnished. On one wall was a sideboard, mahogany with a glass front, full of the cut glass and china he had inherited from his mother along with his sharp features and long limbs. Her picture, in a teak frame carved with an ornate scrolled pattern, stood on top of the sideboard, beside that of his father, a blue-black man with a stern expression. His bed, a simple iron-framed affair draped with a dusty mosquito net, was tucked into the corner furthest from the door. There was a mahogany wardrobe for his clothes and a white food safe. He had no chairs for visitors. In the last six months he had had no visitors.

Close to the foot of the bed a wooden Demerara window opened to the back yard.

On the opposite wall, the slatted windows at either side of the glass-paned front door looked out on Duke Street, a busy thoroughfare that cut across the city from east to west and nearly divided it into uptown and downtown—though most people reckoned that one block north, Park Street, was a better line of demarcation. On his end of it, Duke tended to the seedy and poor. A downmarket drug store, a dark bar, a joiner's furniture shop, a snack and tea shop and a corner dry goods shop-cum-rumshop faced his modest cream and brown façade; upstairs was a wang where men gathered to gamble illegally and drink illegal bush rum, and women followed them to sell other more tactile but similarly illegal wares.

A narrow alley ran beside his front door. It was into this alley he and the boy Clarence now ducked, squinting in the sudden darkness of the short gap. It opened into a swept dirt yard.

The yard was about thirty feet by sixty, and small shrubs sprouted along the limestone boundary wall. Opposite that wall was the wooden back of Sonny's own apartment. Running perpendicular to that was a row of rooms, each with one solid wooden Dutch door and a window only as wide as a man's shoulders. There were five rooms, each housing one family. At the other end of the yard there was another identical row, the whole enclosing the yard like a fist.

Around the central courtyard were the detritus of ten families. A stone clothes bleach, comprising a heap of rocks in the middle of the yard, dominated the scene. It was topped with blindingly white sheets and pillowcases. In front of each door was a small table, in various states of repair depending on which door you looked at, topped with objects like enamel bowls, iron pots, tin pans, a blackened coal pot, a heavy flat iron. The far wall also boasted a rusting galvanized steel enclosure with three doors. One concealed a shower. The other two opened to outhouses.

A standpipe, with a rusty bucket beneath it to catch the drips that ran all day and night, occupied a small, mossy concrete plateau next to the shower.

It was next to this standpipe that a tall woman was bent over a steel tub rubbing clothes against a wooden washboard. Her hair was tied in a blue rag; under it her face was a study in concentration. Her thin, white cotton dress was tucked into her panties at the sides, leaving the dress rucked into a blousy pouch in the front, hiding her figure. But judging from the hard brown arms that emerged from the ragged cap sleeves, Sonny instinctively felt her body was as thin as her son's.

At the sound of their footsteps, she looked up. A fleeting, frightened look skipped across her face before she made it carefully blank.

"And I tell you not to play with that cork ball? You too damn harden," she said, wiping her dripping hands in the gathered fabric of her dress before modestly pulling it out of the tucks at her sides. "Bring your dry ass here and—"

"Madam, is alright. The boy ain't do nothing," Sonny said, handing his charge over to her.

"How you mean, nothing? I see him break the blasted window—"

"No, is all right. I go fix it."

For the first time, she thought to look into her son's face.

"What you crying for?" She turned to Sonny. "You cut his ass already?" The question wasn't angry, just matter-of-fact. It wasn't uncommon for another adult to discipline a child in his parent's absence. In fact, it was encouraged.

Clarence ducked his head. Sonny saw his tears start to flow once more.

"The boy had a shock. He now see a dead man down in the river."

"A dead man! What stupidness you talking? Clarence?" She turned to her son, puzzled over the story. "Clarence, what this mister saying?"

"Madam?" Sonny tried to interject.

"Stop calling me madam. I's a miss."

"Miss, I was really following him to cut his ass but then he bounce up this dead man in the Dry River and I bring him back home. I don't find you should beat him now. He get a shock," he repeated. "Is really all right about the glass, I go pay for it. Is all right. Is just one pane," he said, softly. Clarence was sobbing now. "Why you don't take him inside? Give him some tea, with plenty sugar if you have it. It good for shock. Miss."

She nodded, taking Clarence by the hand into the second door behind Sonny's room. Before she shut the door behind them he glimpsed a rough wooden bed and a bench made from a packing crate, standard furnishing for rooms like these.

"Ah. Miss?" Sonny said to the closing door. The woman put her head back out over the shut bottom half. "I wouldn't force him to talk about it if I was you. Let him sleep if he could. Give him something to eat. He go be fine. Miss—"

"Vero. I's Vero."

"Miss Vero."

"Not Miss Vero. Just Vero. What your name is?"

"Johnson, but they does call me Sonny."

"Thank you, Johnson-but-they-does-call-me-Sonny," she said, with a little smile. Then she shut the top door firmly. Sonny heard the rusty bolt slide home.

He turned back to go to his room, not wanting to face Inspector McLeod in his scruffy home clothes.

He had left the door open but no one had come in. There was little to take, anyway. The bentwood rocker, the iron bed. A little white safe standing in four milk tins full of water to keep ants from getting in. Inside the safe were a stick of butter, a tin of sardines, half a loaf of butter bread and three spotted, overripe bananas. His clothes he kept in the mahogany press next to the bed. They weren't many. Hanging in the tall wardrobe were one dusty black suit made of gabardine, three uniforms, already pressed, and two white shirts with slightly frayed cuffs. His shoes, two pairs, stood underneath the press. They were identical, black patent leather, not service issue but specially made. He kept them shining like mirrors. He had only one vanity and those fancy shoes were it.

Sonny took a shirt and the suit pants off their hangers, shucking his home clothes and replacing them with the more respectable outfit. Then he put on clean socks and shoes.

When he left the room this time, he locked the door behind him.

CHAPTER THREE

Inspector Patrick McLeod was a small, nervous looking white man whose reputation for fairness was well deserved. He would go all out for his men. McLeod had kept Sonny from being fired outright for his insubordination—though he couldn't keep him from being suspended. Disobeying orders was high treason in the force. It just wasn't done. Nothing McLeod could have said to the commissioner of police on Sonny's behalf would have kept him on the job.

The inspector's khaki suit was immaculate, as usual. The white Hardee hat strapped under his chin shaded him from the worst of the sun but his face was still red. The heat outside was murderous.

Sonny cautiously slipped down into the Dry River, retracing the path he had already taken once that day in pursuit of Clarence.

He spotted the party of policemen easily. There was McLeod, red-faced, and two other uniformed constables. Sonny recognized the final member of the party as Sergeant Paul Sandy, his immediate superior under McLeod when he had been assigned to the Besson Street station himself.

The body still lay facedown in the trickling river.

"Stone!" McLeod called. "How the devil did you get involved in this?"

"Inspector. Sergeant. Constables." They returned the greetings silently, nodding once before turning back to the dead man. "I was chasing a little boy who broke a window in my house. He led me to the river. We found the body."

"When did this happen?" McLeod asked. He was born in Ireland but his accent, after more than 20 years as a Trinidadian policeman, was more local than brogue. "When did you find him?"

"Just before I sent to call you, sir. I took the boy home first. He was upset."

"Yes," McLeod said, nodding in agreement. "Good choice. Any idea who this gentleman is?" he added, indicating the body with a flick of the baton he carried in his right hand. It was part of the inspector's uniform and he used it for emphasis, a stage prop for real life.

"I haven't seen the face but I would guess he's the calypsonian. Lord something-or-other. The one who had the song last year about being half Spanish and half African." The corpse's curly hair gave it away as racially mixed; the fancy suit and slick guitar pointed to his profession. There weren't that many calypsonians of mixed race. They tended to be African.

"Jaguar," interjected one of the constables. "The Mighty

Jaguar. The song was 'Zulu Zapata'. And you late. He had a next hit this year again, singing about the scandal in the governor mansion."

Sonny tilted his head as he thought. Yes, there was some vague memory of the song. The governor's cock was in a fight and it lost to a black cock with a long spur... something like that, anyway.

"So, what are we going to do about this Jaguar? Seems someone's tamed him, but good," said McLeod, with a tight smile. "Evers," he called to one of the constables, "run and fetch the M.E. Someone has to call this bastard dead before we can move him. And Constable Geoffrey, see if you can get those tossers in the mortuary to come collect him before he bursts. Damn this heat," he muttered, wiping the back of his neck with a limp white kerchief. "I hate the rain but dry season can be a devil of a time."

He turned to Sonny. "What the hell have you been doing with yourself? You look a bit soft." He poked Sonny's concrete-hard midsection with his baton. "Packing in the food now you're on suspension?"

Sonny grinned, forgetting the dead body for a second or two. "No sir. I do my calisthenics like usual. And I have started running. In fact, I think I have lost weight, rather than put on."

"Well." McLeod was grinning back at him. "Good man." He rubbed his own belly ruefully. "Wish I had half your discipline. But who can lose weight with all this blinking wonderful food around? Stewed smoked herring and two hops bread is hardly an ideal breakfast for me but..." He shrugged and turned back to the body at their feet.

"What do you think happened?"

Sonny considered for a minute. "I think he was attacked up there—" he indicated the bank on the Piccadilly Street side— "and tried to run away using a shortcut through the river. But he collapsed, breaking his guitar. He died here," Sonny concluded.

"You know," said McLeod, grinning even more widely, "no matter how many times you do that I'll never get over it. How the devil do you surmise that?"

The suspended policeman pointed to the body. "See, he's still holding the guitar. Which I doubt he'd do if he had been killed somewhere else and dumped. And the stones next to the body? The tracks running up the bank are full of those. I brought down a heap myself each time I scrambled down the bank today.

"And I don't think this was robbery. That guitar is expensive. And the body is still wearing a ring."

McLeod glanced at the corpse. "What ring?"

The hand that had worn the ruby pinky ring was naked.

"Well, it had been wearing one when we saw it earlier," Sonny amended. "I imagine someone took a liking to it and helped themselves. I couldn't stand watch. I had to—"

"Yes, you told me about the boy," McLeod said, still musing about the things Sonny had guessed about the dead body. "Stabbed, would you say?"

"Yes," Sonny said, without hesitation. "You couldn't go far with a slit throat. And who could hang on to a guitar when someone was trying to chop them with a cutlass?"

"Hmm." McLeod exhaled hard and turned his back to the corpse. "You haven't lost your touch. I bet you anything you're right."

Sonny lifted his shoulders, both accepting the compliment and admitting that he had no control over his gift. He just knew how to put the pieces together, that's all.

"Man, just say you're wrong. Just tell them you're wrong

and you could come back in a second," McLeod said, in a rush. He was talking under his breath. Sergeant Sandy, who had been walking the riverbed looking for clues to what had happened, was out of earshot. "Just say you were wrong and come back."

Sonny tightened his lips and shook his head. "I wasn't wrong."

McLeod sighed again, in exasperation. It wasn't the first time he had bounced his head on Sonny's stubbornness. "Look, you'd best stick around. We'll need to take a statement from you when the M.E.'s through."

"Yes, I thought as much," Sonny replied. A movement up on the bank caught his eye and he remembered that he owed an urchin a penny for fetching the police to the riverbed. "Mind if I take a little walk?"

"Sure, just don't go too far," McLeod agreed.

Sonny looked for a track up the bank that wasn't too steep. He cursed under his breath at the gravel scuffing his shiny shoes. He wasn't vain about much, could give less than a tinker's damn about his clothes and looks, but by God he liked his shoes shiny. It would take work to get the Dry River's dirt off this pair.

The urchin's uncombed head of hair bobbed into view. "You have it?"

"Yes," said Sonny, as he cleared the top of the track. "Come and get it."

As the young boy came into reach, Sonny grabbed him and stuck his hand in the boy's pocket. He pulled out the ruby ring.

"Aye!" shouted the boy. "Tha's mines!" He scuffled with Sonny for a moment. They painted a ridiculous picture, this tall tall man and this small small boy fighting. Sonny locked one of his massive arms around the boy's skinny, flailing ones.

"No, it's that man's down there. This is yours." Sonny thrust the thick copper penny into the boy's balled fist. "Take it."

Reluctantly he opened his hand and took the penny he had bargained for.

"And your mother never tell you not to thief? Shame on you," Sonny scolded the boy. Though he hung his head, Sunny had a feeling the urchin was hardly sorry. He scampered away when Sonny gave him a little push, disappearing into the streets of the city.

Shaking his head, Sonny reflected that it might not have been the boy's fault. Many of these children on the streets were unsupervised by day, running in and out of trouble while their fathers and mothers were at work. And when the night came, they were hardly better off. From the time he hit twelve a boy was considered old enough to run the streets at night. It was a recipe for miscreants and thugs but no one was doing anything about it.

Still thinking about the ragged boy, Sonny started walking along the side of the river. There it was, a patch of rusty brown. Just there, Sonny imagined, The Mighty Jaguar met his match. Even as he stooped over the grass to look at the congealed blood, a crowd began to gather. Apparently, the boy had run straight into the first yard he could and told everybody about the corpse in the Dry River. Soon there was a gathering of some considerable size, jostling at the bank, trying to see what the body looked like.

"Who it is?" a bold woman asked Sonny. He ignored her. "Aye, mister, I did ask you a question. Who it is dead there?"

Sonny got to his feet, dusted his hands and deliberately turned away. Behind him, the woman steupsed, expressing her disgust in a wordless suck of her back teeth. "Some beast feel they is people, eh?" she said, to no one and everyone.

He just walked away. As the people gathered, they began to talk amongst themselves, speculating on the identity of the dead man, the circumstances of how he happened to be lying dead in the Dry River. Sonny even heard someone saying the suit looked familiar. At that, he looked into the faces of the crowd. Most wore expressions of naked curiosity. A few were aghast.

Only one looked saddened: the cocoa brown face of a well-dressed woman with naturally curly hair.

As he watched, her eyes filled with tears. She mouthed a single word, which Sonny couldn't quite make out. It looked like "Len," but he couldn't be sure. He took a step towards her. She saw him, jumped back and melted into the crowd. By the time Sonny had pushed his way through to where she had been standing, she had vanished.

CHAPTER FOUR

The sun was dropping in the sky by the time the medical examiner and the morgue truck pulled up. The doctor, a florid white man in a charcoal suit that had seen better days, took a glance at The Mighty Jaguar's corpse and pronounced him dead. He casually indicated to Constable Evers, who had fetched him at his Henry Street office, to flip the body over. Evers did so with a grunt. Though Jaguar wasn't a fat man, he was solidly built—and being deadweight didn't help the situation. Jaguar's dead hand never let go of the neck of the broken guitar.

His pearl grey sharkskin suit was beyond repair. He had been stabbed in the chest at least five times that Sonny could count. The wounds, judging from the slashed jacket, were inflicted with something wider than a razor, perhaps a kitchen knife, Sonny thought. Once pink, the body's lips were now bluish-white. He had bled to death in the meagre trickle of the Dry River.

Sonny had seen a dead body or six in his time, mostly those of old people who had died peacefully at home. There was one time he had seen a woman whose husband had beaten her to death with a hammer. That had been messy. This, in comparison, was much cleaner.

A low aroma, like meat going bad, was beginning to rise from the body. If Sonny had to guess he would have said Jaguar had died just before dawn. It was now close to half-past-four in the afternoon. Sonny glanced up. Sure enough, the wheeling carrion crows, corbeaux, had begun their spiraling vigil high in the air over the river.

McLeod signaled to the morgue attendants to cover the body and take it away. They laid a thick white canvas over it, put it on a stretcher and shoved it without ceremony into the back of the low, covered lorry that functioned as a meat wagon. Jaguar was on his way to his last performance.

Sonny followed McLeod and the rest of the policemen to the Besson Street station. Two blocks from the river, the station was a beautiful old building that had stood guard over the eastern entrance to the city for fifty years, its high, arched doorways giving a graceful aspect to what was really dirty work. Besson Street swept up the city's dregs, its drunks and whores, its petty thieves and angry young men. This murder would be big news. Sonny wasn't surprised to see a reporter from the Guardian newspaper standing by the door waiting for McLeod.

"Nothing to report, Marks," McLeod told the young, light-skinned boy pre-emptively.

"Not even a name for me yet, Inspector?" The boy, who must have been around twenty-four, asked in a cajoling tone.

Though he was young, he didn't look green. He had kept his notebook in his back pocket, expecting that McLeod would say nothing at this early pass.

"Tell you what. Come back in two hours and we'll have something for you. And," McLeod said blandly, "it's awfully hot out there today. When you come back don't forget to bring yourself a drink."

Hiding his smirk as soon as it came to his lips, the young reporter tipped his brown fedora and walked away, going west.

"Nice boy," McLeod said to Sonny. "Knew his mother a few years ago. What a lady." From his expression Sonny guessed they were more than friends.

They gratefully entered the cool of the station. McLeod took off his hat and ushered Sonny into his little office. It was cluttered with files, newspapers, books and, incongruously, a pair of tall riding boots. "Don't stand on ceremony, my boy. Have a seat. Evers!" he called to the constable, who had gone to the desk at the door of the station.

The constable stuck his head into the room. "Sir?"

"Make me a cup of tea. And bring the forms to me. I'll take his statement."

Evers nodded and went to fulfill the requests. In a moment he had brought in the forms, which he put on McLeod's desk. He went back outside, pulling in but not shutting the door.

Sonny glanced around the room. It had been months since he had been in here. And the last time he had been standing at attention, biting back his fury. Now he looked around calmly. The walls of the little office were decorated with certificates from Scotland Yard, a memorandum in recognition of McLeod's appointment to the Trinidad Police Force, a citation for courage under fire. Above a filing cabinet overflowing with yellowing papers, McLeod had mounted a framed photograph of his first batch of men. Sonny knew that if he looked carefully he would have seen his own face in the unsmiling ranks. He had been twenty-four then and full of hope. Now not so much hope remained. His face wasn't much different, though. He had aged well, he knew without vanity. Many men of thirty-three were lined and grizzled from too much rum and too many cares. While he had had his share of both, something in Sonny's disposition or his gene pool made him weather them better than most.

A little window high on the eastern wall opened to a view of the Laventille hills. Sonny looked without expression at the scene of his downfall. It was in the green and inviting heights above the city he had met his first love. And there, too, he had committed the act of insubordination that had cost him his job.

McLeod brought him back to the office with a strangled clearing of his throat. "So. What time did you say this happened?" He was holding a pen over the form, a tedious but necessary part of police work.

"About two o'clock, I'd say."

"Tell me what happened, in your own words."

"I was at home, at fifteen Duke Street, Port of Spain, alone, when a boy who lives in the barrack yard behind my apartment broke my window. He was playing rounders, I think, with some neighborhood boys."

"Little ruffian. Go on." McLeod was scribbling hard and fast. Sonny waited until the man's gold fountain pen slowed down before he continued.

"I ran out of the house in pursuit of them—they had fled—and followed one, the boy named Clarence, the one who lives behind my apartment, down into the Dry River. The boy found the body first.

"I took him back to Duke Street to his mother, who was at home at the time. She is a washerwoman," he added. "On the way there I stopped an urchin and promised him a penny if he would fetch you to the body. He did. I changed my clothes and returned to the river."

"Right-o," murmured McLeod. "And you've never met this man before today? Had nothing to do with the body, er, being there, as it were?"

Sonny chuckled. "No, sir. First time I met him he was already too dead for introductions."

"So how the devil did you know—or could you guess, at any rate, since we haven't yet confirmed anything—his identity? You said he was a calypsonian."

Sonny explained how he had worked out the man's identity from his clothes and appearance. McLeod was once again impressed, shaking his head in respect. "Boggles the mind how you do it, man. Evers!" he bawled out again. "Where's that bloody tea?"

Evers hustled in with a pot and two cups on a tray. "Had was to boil the water, Inspec."

"Yes, of course you did. Evers, did you ever meet Johnson Stone? Constable, just like you. Unfortunately, on suspension but a good man, all the same."

From the time Sonny looked into Evers' face he knew his reputation had preceded him. The other constable's thick lips curled into a sneer before he could hide the expression of contempt. "And you's the one with the Shangos and them up in the hills?" Evers asked, a paragon of disdain.

"Yes," Sonny said, quietly, meeting and holding the younger man's gaze until Evers dropped his eyes and blushed.

"Anything else, Inspector?" Evers asked, turning to his boss.

"Yes, as a matter of fact. Get out on the street and find out what you can about this Jaguar. Real name, address, what he did when he wasn't singing calypso, if he had any enemies. That sort of thing."

"You might want to ask around at Piccadilly and Duke," Sonny said. "I saw a woman in the crowd who looked like she could have been his sister."

"Oh? You didn't mention that," McLeod said, his pale grey eyes alighting on Sonny, who just shrugged again.

"She came too quickly for it to be much further away than that," Sonny said. "And I would hazard a guess that he was killed close to home."

"Jesus, Mary and Joseph. One day you have to teach me how to do that," muttered McLeod. "Well, you heard him, Evers. Start at Piccadilly and Duke." Without saying anything else he dismissed Evers with a wave of the hand.

Sonny sat in silence for a moment before he spoke. "They've been talking about me."

"Station gossip, nothing more," McLeod said, dismissing the rumors as easily as he had dismissed the junior officer. "Nobody knows what really happened up there, you know. All we know is that the Shangos should have gone to jail, all of them, for breaking the Ordinance. You've never told me why you let that girl go against Sandy's orders."

Sonny didn't reply. He looked up at Laventille and said nothing.

"Well. I suppose that's that, then. Well, Constable Stone, all I can say is don't leave town." McLeod winked at him. He picked up the teapot and slid open a drawer beneath his desk, from which he fished a bottle of Irish whiskey. "Fancy a spot of tea?"

CHAPTER FIVE

Though he outweighed Inspector McLeod by half, at least, the small Irishman lived up to his ethnic reputation and could out-drink Sonny twice over. By the time the sun was going down over Port of Spain, Sonny was much mellower than he had been two hours before when he walked into the Besson Street police station. The warm glow in his belly wasn't just the joy at renewing an old acquaintance—though he had enjoyed reminiscing with McLeod about his early adventures in the force—but owed more to the fine Irish whiskey with which McLeod insisted on spiking their three pots of tea.

Evers, the police constable McLeod had sent out into the city to find information on their dead calypsonian, was just walking in when Sonny was walking out. The other man watched Sonny cut eye and gave a little snort of derision as he brushed past him on his way to the Inspector's office. Sonny contemplated going in behind him, just to assuage his curiosity about the corpse's real name and last place of abode, but reconsidered. The man known in calypso circles as The Mighty Jaguar was dead. Stabbed to death on the eastern bank of the Dry River. Whatever his business had been, it would keep until tomorrow.

The setting sun oozed magnificence. It was an incandescent orange ball sinking over the low buildings of the city, spilling tangerine and magenta color into the fluffy banks of clouds that surrounded it. The waters of the Gulf of Paria were stained blood red by the sunset, reminding Sonny of the sunlight streaming through the red pane of glass in his apartment earlier that day. Which, in turn, reminded him that he needed to get a pane replaced. He'd already promised Clarence's mother he'd pay for it himself, not wanting her to beat the money's worth out of her son's backside. Though he was in a harsh profession, he was by nature a gentle man. Sonny especially had a soft spot for children and dogs, though he himself owned neither. But other people's, well, he could love those fiercely without taking them home.

Though the glazier he knew in Woodbrook would be long gone from his shop by now, Sonny decided to take a walk to the suburb on the other side of the city. Bobby "Glass" Hackett sometimes worked late, his passion for his work tying him to the shed behind his house. Besides, he knew if Glass wasn't in his shop he wouldn't be far; the glazier's nickname wasn't just because of his profession but because he always had a glass in his hand. His bar of choice was on Tragarete Road, not far from his house.

Sonny's long legs carried him briskly along Marine Square, the long promenade that formed the heart of the city. The financial district, upscale shopping center and the city's biggest church, the Cathedral of the Immaculate Conception, were all either on or radiated from Marine Square. Not that Sonny was watching the sights. As he passed the imposing Gothic cathedral, its yellow limestone turning golden in the setting sun's still-hot rays, his mind was far behind him. It was, to be precise, on the paved bed of the Dry River where Jaguar had breathed his last.

Though it wasn't unusual for a calypsonian to be involved in a fracas here or there—and some built solid reputations on their fighting prowess—it was unusual for one to be stabbed to death. Was it over a woman? Was it some petty money dispute gone bad? What exactly was the reason for the five deep slits with which Jaguar had been ventilated sometime that morning? And who, Sonny thought to himself, was the woman on the riverbank who had cried for the slain singer? She looked like Jaguar, had the same complexion and same curly hair, but that wasn't necessarily saying anything, despite the confident lead he had given his former superior officer at the police station. She could have been his lover, his wife, his neighbor or just a fan.

Calypsonians on the whole were a loved species. They were by parts crusaders, poets and storytellers, griots like in the old African tradition his Toco grandmother used to describe, telling the tribe's story to future generations. But they were court jesters, too, whose intricate lyrics could bring a smile to even the most somber face. Jaguar, if it was indeed he who had met his end in the river that morning, had been among the jesters, using humorous lyrics to make a point and win a following. The only song of his that Sonny knew well was "Zulu Zapata", a parody on the ill will between black and white people. Jaguar claimed to be half Spanish and half black, a claim borne out by his wavy curls. The song posited that if he had to pick a side he wouldn't know which to choose. "If a Spanish had to catch a slave, I would be on the horse and hiding in the cave," the chorus went.

"Spanish" was a confusing term to Sonny, in this instance. Did Jaguar mean that he was half Spanish as in actual Spanish from Spain, one of the thousands of Europeans who had immigrated to the island as indentured workers after the Emancipation of African slaves? Or was he using the local term, which could refer to a Venezuelan from "down the Main", who could be full-blooded European or mestizo, mixed with African and Amerindian? Jaguar's swelling features had given no clue.

The song had been a big hit, bringing Jaguar close to winning Road March in last year's Carnival. It had been on everybody's lips up until the last moment. Then "Happy Wanderer" had swept in out of the blue and stolen the victory from Jaguar as the most played tune in the festival's street parade. This year Jaguar had come back strong, with a song about a cockfight in the governor's mansion, a song which many said wasn't fiction but alluded to a scandalous liaison between the governor's wife and a black man.

Sonny didn't know the song. Since his suspension from the police force he had been inside more than out, virtually ignoring Carnival that February in favor of retreating to his family home on the northeast coast. After his last meeting with the commissioner at the police barracks in St James, when he was once again sent home without being reinstated, Sonny had given away his meagre groceries, packed a small suitcase and headed for home.

Trinidad's sun sets fast, and though he'd only been walking about ten minutes it was already deep dusk. His long-legged stride had taken him to the edge of the downtown district already. The daytime people, shopkeepers and their assistants, tradesmen, stevedores and the like, were hurrying home, having tarried long past their four o'clock whistles. The city's night shift was coming out. These were fast women and hard men, those who lived for the pleasures of the wang, the club, the bar. Among those lean and hungry faces, Sonny's air of distraction stood out like a daisy in a bed of stinging nettle.

Sonny was oblivious to the glances he got as he briskly ate the miles from the city to Woodbrook, a suburb of middle-class black and brown folk, past the area known as Corbeau Town. He had already passed the docks and decided to go up Shine Street, emerging on Park Street by the low back wall of the Lapeyrouse Cemetery. The old resting place of the planter elite held no terrors for Sonny. As a child he'd been amazed at how frightened his peers were of graves and cemeteries. They would run screaming if they had to go near a graveyard. Sonny, on the other hand, instinctively knew that the dead weren't the ones you had to worry about.

Glass' workshop and home were on Roberts Street, a block from the cemetery. The tiny gingerbread cottage, a Victorian home with fancy wooden fretwork all around the eaves, a deep bay window and a demure front porch sporting comfortable planter's chairs, was surrounded by a lush garden. Bougainvillea, deep purple intertwined with white, spilled over the low wall separating the property from the road. Glass was no gardener; his wife Marie had a green thumb. Sonny knew that at the back of the house she had planted mango, cherry and citrus trees which provided fresh fruit and shade. Glass kept strictly away from the plants. He would often say that all bush was good for was walking on.

It was full dark by the time Sonny reached their wrought iron gate. The light in Glass' workshop was out so Sonny knew he would either be in the house or at Tim's Restaurant and Bar, a rumshop on Tragarete Road, which ran parallel to Roberts Street, a block away. He stood outside the gate and called his friend's nickname.

Marie, a petite black woman with black hair and golden skin, opened the front door nearly instantly. "Aye aye! Since when do you stand up and call? What the jail is this?" she said, mockingly. "Come inside!"

Sonny sheepishly opened the gate and went up the steps into the little house. Glass was as small as his wife, who couldn't have been taller than five foot four, and around them in their dolly house, Sonny felt a giant. He bent at the waist to kiss Marie's talcum-dusted cheek. "Miss Marie, how you?"

"Comme ci, comme ça," she said. "And you? What brings you down here at this hour?" Though it couldn't have been past seven, Sonny knew, it was late by his recent standards. In the last six months he'd become such a recluse that evenings found him indoors, not out visiting these old friends.

"Damn fool boy in my yard break my window," he grunted.

"And this is the hour you come for a replacement? Friendship is friendship but—" Marie said, jokingly fierce. "Too besides, that worthless man is not even here. Oh, come and sit down," she invited, pulling him down into one of the solid wooden chairs on the porch. "Lime or cherry?" she asked, flitting inside.

"Surprise me!" he responded, raising his voice to be heard through the exquisitely beveled glass panes set in the cypre front doors. Cream lace curtains shielded the interior of the house from his gaze but he knew from past experience what lay inside. A low-slung Morris set, polished and stained nearly black was the centerpiece, its solidity counterpointed by shelves and shelves of glass objects which Marie's husband liked to blow for her. They ranged from tiny blobs defying classification to graceful birds and perfect human forms. Glass was no expert—he didn't have the right tools or the right materials, he always complained—but he knew what to do with some molten glass.

Marie came back outside with two tall glasses of frothy pink liquid. "Cherry and lime," she said, with a cheeky grin. She handed one to him and took a seat in the chair opposite to his. "Now tell me the real reason you've come down at here this hour of the night."

CHAPTER SIX

Sonny took a sip of his cherry and lime drink. It was tangy and full of pulp, which gritted pleasantly on his teeth as it flowed into his mouth. The shards of ice in the glass were already melting, so Sonny stuck in his finger and stirred it a bit. It wasn't good manners, but then good friends didn't mind bad manners now and then, he thought. He popped the finger into his mouth.

"How does it taste? D'you like it?"

"What! Yeah, man. Boss. Capital," he said, taking another sip. It had been a longish walk from Besson Street, about two miles. He only recognized he was thirsty when he had had the tall glass thrust upon him.

"The real reason?" Marie prompted again.

"Huh. Let a man drink his juice, nah," he prevaricated. Marie was the size of a terrier, with about as much tenacity. He knew she wouldn't let it go until he talked.

"Found a dead body today. In the river."

She nearly gagged on her juice. "But I thought you were on suspension? They put you back on and you didn't say anything to us?"

"No, no, you know I would have tell you and Glass if that did happen. No, I was just by the river—chasing a boy who break my blasted window—when we see the body." In fact, if he had found the body on the job, he wouldn't have told her anything about it. He liked to keep his work and home life separate. Sometimes that worked against him, he reflected grimly.

"Who was it? Do you know yet?" Marie asked. She didn't ask with prurience like the gawking bystanders had shown earlier today around the body. She asked because it was clear Sonny needed to get the story off his chest.

Marie DeFour, as she had been before she married the man who had become Sonny's best friend, was everything Sonny was not. He had grown up in the bush, on a cocoa plantation in Grande Riviere; she had been born and reared in Woodbrook. She had been educated at the feet of Catholic nuns in a convent school in town; his stern and forbidding father and paternal grandmother had schooled him, with Milton, the Bible and Charles Dickens as texts. Marie was small; Sonny was big. She was honey-brown; he was sloe black. She was firmly middle-class, daughter of a schoolmaster and a seamstress; he, although raised in a wealthy family, in his attitudes, usual choice of language and perspective had more in common with the peons who picked and danced the cocoa than the property-owning class to which he technically belonged.

When Sonny had come to town twelve y   T
had been one of the first people he'd met.
fallen in love with her instantly, with her d   wit
her flashing wit, he soon met her steady b(
liked him too much to pursue her behir
back. They had stayed friends, all three, through Mari
Glass' marriage ten years ago, and Sonny's joining the police
that year, giving up a life of indolence that had begun to pall.
They had become a foursome when he'd met Joan. But when
that was over, as it soon was, it was the three of them once
more.

She was still waiting for his answer.

"Not sure. I think it's that calypsonian, Jaguar." He lapsed
into silence again. His black eyes were miles away.

Marie left him to his silence, drinking her homemade
blend and looking at him without speaking.

She loved him, in her way. He was one of the kindest
and sweetest people she knew, she thought. Funny that a
man like that had ended up in such a brutal profession. But
when he came up from the bush at twenty-one, flush with
money and not a clue what to do with it, she had watched
him go from pillar to post before settling down into something
he was really good at. Sonny's mind loved puzzles. He was
always turning things over, people, places, events, looking
for the connections and bridges between things. In another
time, in another place, had he been another man—a white
one—he could have written his own ticket as a detective, she
thought. But this was Trinidad, in the Thirties. The colonial
government did not encourage initiative among members
of the African race. He could be a policeman but wouldn't
rise about the rank of sergeant, and that only if he worked
three times as hard as one of the British men the colonial
government brought to the island as officers. There were
some good men on the force, at all levels, but few were as
good as Sonny, she felt.

though she did love him, and he had turned her head with his smooth good looks and exquisitely gentle manner for about five minutes when they first met, she felt he was like a brother to her and Glass. Their friendship was one of the most enduring and fulfilling parts of her life. Both men loved their work; she was just content to stay at home and putter with her plants. She was no career woman and, though she sometimes envied the financial independence of other women who worked for a living, she didn't envy them the stress of raising a family and holding down a job. As soon as she had become pregnant with her son Jacob shortly after her marriage, she had quit her job as a doctor's receptionist and become a housewife.

Now she, Jacob and Glass lived comfortably on what Glass made as one of the few glaziers on the island. Though he wasn't an artisan on the scale of the Italian masters who still had to provide stained windows and leaded panes to local churches, Glass was very good at what he did and had developed a reputation as one of the best in Trinidad. He had taken on an apprentice a few years ago, passing on his skills to the next generation although he had many years left to work before he would consider retiring and leaving the business to Jacob.

Like Glass and Marie, Sonny adored Jacob, who was spending the night at his maternal grandmother's home a few blocks away. The boy was everybody's saltfish, a favorite because of his perky enthusiasm and way with words. Though he was only nine, he even had an eye for the ladies and Sonny would often sit with him in the front porch passing comments on every respectable woman who walked by, and some not-so-respectable ones, too. But that was before Sonny had sunk into the despair of the past six months.

She drank the last of her juice and cleared her throat noisily. Sonny looked up, wounded eyes startled out of reverie. "Do you want to wait or do you want to go and get

Glass? Though," she added with a wry grin, "if I send you to the rumshop behind him there's no guarantee I would see either of you for hours yet."

Sonny laughed loudly, polished off his drink and got to his feet. "I go go and get him. Don't worry, we go come back just now."

He handed her the glass, slick with condensation, pinkish dregs forming a puddle at the bottom along with a last sliver of melting ice. She stood up and watched him walk out of the yard into the Woodbrook night.

"Joan, you bitch, you have no idea what you've done," she muttered to his distant back.

CHAPTER SEVEN

Stepping out into the cooling air, Sonny took a deep breath before he set off to Tim's Restaurant and Bar. A rumshop by any other name, a slight Chinese man named Tim See Sing, and his wife, a buxom black woman named Dulcie, ran it. Though they never spoke to each other in the shop and operated on some kind of magical non-verbal system of communication, Tim and Dulcie had managed to produce about a dozen brown babies in the twelve years Sonny had been a regular at their bar.

Though it was called a restaurant, Tim's served mostly rum with water for chaser, selling cutters of fried chicken gizzards, boiled eggs, salted peanuts and seasoned fried channa on the side. When the urge took her, Dulcie would cook up a magnificent pot of pelau or thick split pea sancoche; neither the chicken and rice dish nor the meaty soup would last very long because she had a universally acknowledged sweet hand. Her customers tried to cajole her into selling meals more regularly, saying she had to earn extra money to mind all the chinky-eyed pickney she was turning out, but Dulcie would have none of it. Her standard response was that as long as the men of Woodbrook continued to drink rum she and her children would never go hungry.

Tim's was, like most rumshops in Trinidad, whether in town or in the country, a bar set inside a wide room, its many side-by-side doors open to the road. It was brightly lit, with unadorned metal tables and chairs placed both inside and out on the pavement in front of the wide-open doors. Tim and his wife sold rum from about ten in the morning till the last customer rolled out at night, usually around eleven, though they could go past midnight on a Friday night. Tim, Dulcie and their dozen children lived in two rooms behind the rumshop.

As Sonny walked towards the bar, he spotted Glass with his namesake in hand at a table under the awning in front of the rumshop.

"What! That is you, Sonny?" Glass shouted. "Tim, send your missus with a bottle of rum for me and my test here—" he began to shout over his shoulder. Sonny waved him down.

"Nah, Glass. One drink, but Marie say she want to talk so I promise we wouldn't stay long." He pulled up a chair, which was slightly rickety and uniformly uncomfortable with a deeply sloping back, but all that Tim's had to offer by way of seating. "Tim, just one shot for me," he said. Tim didn't bother to nod, just poured the shot in a short glass and left it on the bar for his wife, equally taciturn, to bring to Sonny's table. "Dulcie, you ain't fed up of that Chineeman yet?" Sonny teased the unsmiling woman when she rolled over to him, hips like a juggernaut.

Slapping the glass to the table, she sucked her teeth. "You go mind all them half-Chinee children?" She sucked her teeth again and rolled back behind the bar.

Still remembering the Irish tea he'd drunk by the pot earlier that evening, Sonny nursed his rum as he and Glass caught up on the happenings of the past month or so since they'd last talked. In the bar, the handful of men sitting around tables with bottles and flasks of rum and water were chatting and laughing raucously. A rumshop was no place for delicacy. It was a place for loud talk and rough humor, hence all the picong that Tim and Dulcie were subjected to.

After a couple of minutes of small talk under the noise of the bar, Glass cut to the chase.

"Why you looking like your mother dead again?" One thing he wasn't, was subtle, that Glass.

Sonny shook his head. "Man," he said, peering into the depths of the amber liquid in the glass, "I bounce up a dead man today. It kinda shake me."

Glass said nothing, but put his own drink to his mouth and downed it in a gulp. "Tim, how much I have for you?"

"You drink three rum?" Tim asked, his Chinese accented tongue touched with a Trinidadian twang. "Fifteen cent. You pay now or you trust?"

Glass, rising from the uncomfortable chair, dipped into his pants pocket for the coins. "I go pay you now. Save the credit for when I ain't have none," he said. They went through the ritual every evening, as Tim did with all his customers, but in truth Glass seldom took his drinks on credit. He reasoned that if he had to have a drink that badly he'd find the money to pay for it, or go without.

Sonny stood too. Head and shoulders taller than his friend, he towered over him, making Glass look a pot-bellied child next to him. But neither man noticed the difference.

They walked out of the bar into the cool night, leaving the loud talk of men in the rumshop behind.

"I really pass because I want to get a glass to replace one of them fancy window you put in my apartment," Sonny began.

"The ones in the door or the ones over the back window?" Glass asked.

"Back window. But—"

"Clear or red?"

"Clear. But—"

"How the ass you manage to break that, Sonny?" Glass asked, annoyed. The dimpled glass wouldn't be hard to replace but it was in an inconveniently high spot. He didn't like heights.

"Not me," Sonny said, growing annoyed at all Glass' interruptions. "The knotty-head boy in the yard behind. Playing rounders or some dotishness. I ain't even know why they was playing rounders with a cork ball, or how it reach so high up. But they break the damn glass, all right?"

"All right. Continue," Glass offered magnanimously.

Sonny paused and reflected that he should perhaps wait until Marie was there to tell the story or he'd end up telling it for the fifth time that day. Fortunately, it was a short walk to the house and before Glass could start harassing Sonny for details they were raising the iron latch of the wrought iron gate.

"Marie, my love!" Glass called to his wife, who had resumed her seat on the porch while waiting for them to come back. They kissed lightly on the lips before Glass went into the house to draw a dining room chair for himself. The diminutive porch was too small to hold more than a pair of the planter's chairs. Settling into his seat, he waved to Sonny, who was leaning a hip on the porch wall by the step. "Sit down, man. Start again with the story."

When he had given them details of his macabre discovery, Marie and Glass exchanged looks.

"Sounds like you're missing your work, Son Son," Marie said, smiling a little. "You're trying to solve this killing but it's not your job right now. If they want you to work on the case they should bring you back, officially," she added.

He grunted.

"You must really be Miss Mary Jackass if you want to work on this thing without being put back on the force," Glass put in.

Sonny grimaced. He knew they meant well. But he was like a dog with a bone when it came to puzzles. This was a puzzle, as fine as any he'd ever seen. Someone had killed a man and Sonny Stone couldn't rest until he knew who and why.

Something was niggling the back of his mind. He turned the feeling over until he realized with a jolt that he still had the dead man's pinkie ring in his pocket. He'd taken it from the urchin on the riverbank and hadn't returned it to Inspector McLeod as procedure demanded. But, as his best friends now reminded him, he wasn't on the force anymore. Damn procedure.

He took the surprisingly weighty object from his pocket and held it in his palm.

"What do you have there?" Marie asked.

"Ruby ring. I see it on the dead man. The ragamuffin I pay to fetch the police pull it off the body before they come. I take it back from him but forget to give McLeod it at the station."

The ring was clearly expensive. Heavy, yellow gold formed a solid setting for a ruby about the size of a large peanut. Around the gemstone were diagonal slashes, almost like a glazier's beveling of glass.

"Let me see! This looks familiar, don't you think so, Bobby?" Marie said, taking the ring from Sonny and showing it to her husband. Glass squinted at it, nodding.

"Can't tell why it looks familiar, though."

Marie was silent for a heartbeat then broke into a grin. "Dunderhead! It's just like my wedding band!" True enough, when she put her wedding band next to the pinkie ring it was clear the same hands had made them. Both were made from that sunny yellow gold, both had gemstones set in solid metal without prongs to hold them in place (except that Marie's was a much smaller diamond), and both were embellished with the diagonal beveling.

"You think is Kumar make this?" Glass said, taking the ring from his wife's small hands and peering at it. "There's something inscribed inside," he said. "'To G. E. Love T.'"

"Well, that helpful," Sonny said, ruefully. "Now if we know who is G.E. and who is T we could go real far."

"Kumar would know," Marie said. "Why don't you ask him—if you intend to pursue this, that is."

Sonny's immediate response was, "Where do I find him?"

CHAPTER EIGHT

The three friends talked late into the night. It was past midnight when Sonny rose to leave. Marie put a hand on his thickly muscled arm to stop him. "Sonny, we have something to tell you." She shot a quick look at her husband before continuing. "We want to buy the house."

Sonny was taken aback. The house, like two others in Woodbrook, including Marie's parents', was legally his property. His father, having made money hand over fist in cocoa at the end of the last century, had invested in real estate in and around Port of Spain. Johnson Stone, Snr, had owned a number of barrack yards in the city as well as the three cottages in Woodbrook. It was the latter which had brought Sonny into Marie's life. When his parents had died within months of each other when he was twenty-one, Sonny ventured into the city to see firsthand what he owned. The schoolmaster's daughter had instantly caught his eye but fate wouldn't allow anything more than friendship. As much a friend to her as to her fiancée, he had given them the use of the tiny cottage on Roberts Street as a wedding present, over their loud protests.

Now, ten years later, they wanted to buy it from him.

"You know is yours as long as you want it," Sonny argued.

"Yes," Glass said. "And we damn grateful for ten years of rent-free accommodation, partner, but look Jacob getting big. I can't be calling myself a man if I sponging off my best friend for he whole life."

In truth, Sonny saw his point. There were things men had to do.

He nodded his head, unsmiling. "I go talk to Peters." Peters, his lawyer, had an office on Abercromby Street in the city. The man saw him about twice a year; agents collected Sonny's rents, took on tenants and saw to the reasonable upkeep of each of his properties, including the massive but increasingly unproductive cocoa estate in Grande Riviere where he had grown up. Cocoa was no longer king and the estate's yield of black gold brought in less and less money with each quarter. Sonny knew a day would come when it would cost more to keep it running than it made. In the meantime, he had more than enough income to live on from the properties he rented out, in addition to his policeman's pay that went untouched into the bank. He lived in the Duke Street apartment because he liked it there. It was reasonably close to his job, quiet and clean. Besides, he had simple tastes. He found the froufrou of the Woodbrook houses, like the cottage he had lent to the Hacketts, appalling. If he couldn't live in the bush, he didn't much care where he lived.

Peters hated the thought of his wealthy client living in squalor in a barrack yard—even if it was a nice one by the city's standards. But how do you argue with such a big, fat retainer? Sonny's grandmother, Elsie, who still lived in Toco in the house her son had built for her, had never seen the apartment. She had packed up some essentials for her grandson—all the mahogany furniture had come from the estate house in Grande Riviere—and washed her hands of it. If he wanted to live like a peasant, so be it.

Peters, at least, would be thrilled that he would finally be making some money off the gingerbread cottage, though Sonny would give his friends the cheapest price their dignity would afford them.

Sonny's background and wealth were a closely guarded secret. He didn't have many friends apart from Marie and Glass, and even his agents didn't know him personally, only dealing with his attorney. The one person he had told was Joan.

On the porch of the home she and her husband would soon own, Marie's eyes shone with pride. "We could go to the bank in the morning!"

Sonny laughed. "I think we could wait a while longer. Let me talk to Peters, work out a price. I promise I go come back when I know what is what."

The couple nodded as one. Glass grasped Sonny's hand tightly. "Good man. Good man."

Reflecting that he hadn't done his calisthenics that day but he'd made up for it with a whole lot of walking, Sonny made his way home through the silent, dark city. It was going on one o'clock when he came to his block of Duke Street. He had already pushed in his door when part of him realized he'd left it locked.

"He reach," a thick voice muttered as the door opened. It was all Sonny needed. He folded his slender, pretty hands into fists and laid into the man who had spoken.

The streetlight outside his door spilled in through the window slats and the half-open door, but the apartment remained only dimly lit. In the semi-darkness, he worked by touch.

He felt other hands grasping at him from both sides but Sonny Stone was nothing if not focused. He pummeled the man until he couldn't feel him moving, and then switched his attention to the men on either side of him.

They were, to their detriment, short and slender, nothing like the wall of muscle that was Sonny. He swung a carefully aimed blow in the semi-darkness and was satisfied at the crack he heard as his fist connected with a jaw. The other man didn't hang around to suffer the same fate. He grabbed the first man to fall and dragged his limp body out the door before Sonny could react.

Reaching for a box of matches to light the hurricane lamp on top of his safe, Sonny took a look at the remaining thug. He was a painfully thin black man with a conk, his kinky hair straightened out with lye and then carefully waved with pomade. In his open mouth a gold tooth gleamed. Sonny slapped his face lightly.

"Get up."

The man groaned. As he came to, he jumped about a foot and tried to scramble up, but only succeeded in banging the back of his head painfully on the pine floor.

"Get up. Slow," Sonny said, squatting next to the man's prostrate body. Though Sonny's voice was mild, the man could see the anger in Sonny's face. The steady, golden light of the hurricane lantern made Sonny's eyes pitch black pools. With his angular features pinched in fury and his massive body coiled to strike, Sonny looked just plain evil.

The man sat up, slowly as Sonny had suggested. He put

his hands at his sides, palms down on the wooden floor.

"Who send you?" Sonny asked. "What you want?"

"B-b-boss," the man stuttered in a low voice, "a-a-all we did want is the ring."

Sonny's eyes, already narrowed, closed for a fraction of a second. The ring. Whoever Jaguar was, he had friends in low places.

"Who send you?"

"B-b-boss, i-if I t-t-tell you that, I d-d-d-dead," the man said.

Sonny grinned. If anything, it made him look even more evil. "Better you tell me now. Either that or I go have to… get it out of you. If you know what I mean."

The man swallowed heavily. He still felt the fire in his jaw where Sonny's fist, as delicate as it looked, had nearly knocked his head off. "I-i-i-if I tell you, y-y-you go let me g-go?"

Sonny shrugged, still grinning. He was giving no quarter to the man who had broken into his home and tried to attack him.

"Perro. That is all I know," the stammering man said.

"Where he hire you?"

"I n-n-never see him," he said, quickly. "Is Mikey and them who tell me was a work to put down tonight. I s-s-s-swear—"

"Get on your feet." Sonny had heard enough. The thug, no more than eighteen, Sonny saw now that he looked, was going to be in enough trouble when this "Perro" realized he had failed to get the ring and had given up his name, to boot. Sonny pushed the slight body out the door. "If I ever see you again I go kill you. Understand?" The boy nodded, fear naked on his face. "Get out of here."

His would-be attacker wasted no time before he bolted out the door and down the street towards the river.

Sonny watched him run, then took a hard look up and down the street, looking for anything suspicious. Satisfied that everything looked normal, he closed and locked his door and turned to see what had been done to his apartment.

The intruders had pulled his clothes to the floor, shredded the ticking of his mattress, smeared butter all over the safe, all in their search for the dead man's ring. Even his half-a-loaf of butter bread was eviscerated, leaving fluffy white dough all over the room. The ants would have a field day with that, Sonny thought in despair.

And he had been worried that he'd be coming home to broken glass on the floor.

Opening the bottom drawer of the wardrobe, he saw at a glance that the men had not discovered the false bottom. He carefully slid it out, revealing a shotgun and a revolver, with several boxes of ammunition. He extracted the revolver, loaded it and undid the safety, slid the compartment back into place and shut the drawer.

He pushed the bentwood rocker back close to the bed, blew out the lantern and sat down to a long night's wait.

The gun was heavy in his hand.

CHAPTER NINE

For the second time that week, Sonny awoke with a start in his bentwood rocker.

This time it wasn't a thump on his wooden apartment wall that jerked him out of sleep, but a hesitant tap on the glass pane of his single door.

His arm and wrist ached with the effort of holding a heavy revolver trained at the very door for six hours. He had not slept long. His eyes were as dry and gravelly as quarry dirt.

Another tap and Sonny shook his head to clear it.

Rising and walking to the door with the stealth of a cat, Sonny peered through the slanting wooden jalousies at his visitor.

It was Clarence, the little boy who'd discovered the body yesterday. And he was holding a wooden waiter covered in a blue plaid tea towel.

As Sonny looked, the boy reached up gingerly to tap on the door again, balancing the tray on one knee with his other hand.

The suspended police constable tucked the blue steel piece into his waistband in the small of his back before unlocking the door. Clarence stood on his front step in the same clothes he'd worn the day before. "Morning. Mammy send this for you. She say was to tell you thanks for bringing me back home yesterday because you could have leave me in the river with the dead man."

Sonny, a small smile tugging at the corner of his stern looking lips, took the tray from the boy. "Tell she I say thanks. And I would have never do that." He uncovered the tray, which was made of smoothly polished wood. It looked old, older than the boy by plenty, of some pale wood with dark red wooden handles. Sonny placed it on the safe, avoiding the smeared butter his housebreakers had left in their wake the night before, and took a bite of the woman's offering.

She had sent him a golden-brown fried bake. The light bread roll, about the size of his cupped palms, was crisp on the outside, with salty, oily cheddar melting in its fluffy, warm interior. Next to it was a blue enamel cup of cocoa, still steaming. A thin scum of cocoa fat floated on top. Sonny hadn't had cocoa tea so smooth and rich with vanilla since he had left his mother's house twelve years before. Somehow people in town didn't have the knack for concocting the drink, which was made of grated cocoa boiled with milk and spices.

His first sip of the drink took Sonny back to his childhood, the cool damp of the cocoa estate and the music of picking season, when the Venezuelan "cocoa payols", in their wide straw sombreros and woolen alpagats, along with Africans and Indians whose indentureship contracts had expired, cut the hard gold and orange pods from the trees. The split pods ended up emptied of their beans, which were covered in sticky white coating small boys like Clarence would eagerly suck for the tart, milky flavor. Piled high, the beans were dried in the sun in the cocoa house, a massive barn with a rolling roof that could be pushed aside to let the harsh heat of the sun burn out a unique flavor from the beans. The cocoa peasants would walk barefoot through the beans, a shuffling step known as dancing the cocoa. When rain threatened, the roof was rolled back to shelter the black gold. Sonny would never forget the smoky, dizzying smell of thousands of pounds of cocoa beans heaped on a floor waiting to be bagged and piled on a donkey cart and, eventually, shipped away to Europe.

Trinidad cocoa, when Sonny was coming up from boyhood, fetched premium prices on the world market. That translated to the best of everything for him and his family. But his grandmother always cautioned him, "You could buy knowledge but wisdom and understanding are priceless." And, he might have added, memory too.

The silky liquid, hot but not scalding, slid down his throat. Clarence was still standing in the doorway, looking at Sonny's mouth chewing the warm bake and cheese. When Sonny took a grateful gulp of cocoa tea, the boy seemed to shudder with desire. Sonny waved him in and pointed to the bed.

"Sit down. Watch out for the glass," he reminded him, drily. Clarence had the grace to blush. The skinny boy sat down on the ragged strips of ticking. Not only had they ripped the mattress apart, the intruders had pulled the brown coconut fiber out of the mattress by handfuls and strewn it on the floor. Clarence, still looking hungrily at Sonny, idly kicked a tuft at his feet.

Sonny took a final bite of the sandwich and handed the uneaten half to the boy. Clarence looked at it, a twitching hand hovering above his lap. "You ain't go tell Mammy?" he asked plaintively.

Sonny chuckled. "No, I ain't go tell your mammy. Take it. And when you done you could drink the cocoa tea."

The lean man stretched his arms towards the white bagasse ceiling, rising to the balls of his feet. He quickly bent over and touched his toes a couple of times, then twisted at the waist with his arms held straight out at his sides. Clarence, his mouth full of bake, mumbled, "Umph hoo woon?"

"I sure your mother tell you not to talk with a full mouth," Sonny said lightly, continuing his exercises.

Clarence gulped noisily. "What you doing?"

"Exercise. Calisthenics. It good for the body. Make you healthy and strong."

Clarence made short work of Sonny's leftover breakfast, watching without any further comment as Sonny moved through a swift sequence of movements. Sitting on the bed, he began to bounce up and down on the destroyed mattress, the bedsprings underneath completely new to him. Sonny had seen his bed yesterday, a poor man's special made of old packing crate slats and padded with rags. It was the usual sleeping arrangement of the poorest class in town, an alternative to sleeping on the floor, which many thought would make them catch a cold.

As he twisted and jumped lightly, Sonny thought. The boy could come in handy that morning.

"Boy, you want to help me do something?"

Clarence nodded, his mud brown eyes twinkling.

"I have to go and bathe but I don't want to pass in front and I don't want nobody to see me. You could pass a bucket of water through the window for me?"

Sonny's back window was a large wooden Demerara affair that swung up and out on a hinge. It could be held open by a length of wood.

Again, Clarence nodded. Sonny handed him a white enamel pail he fished out from under the bed. The boy slipped through the window and filled the pail at the standpipe in the yard then passed it to Sonny over the windowsill. A little cold water slopped from the bucket but Sonny didn't mind the puddle. The whole apartment was a wreck anyway, between the clumps of coconut fiber, shredded mattress ticking, broken glass, strewn clothes and smeared butter.

"Clarence," Sonny said to the boy, who still waited uncertainly outside the window, "let me close this and I go call you when I done bathe off."

He slipped the wooden post that held the window open and bolted the window shut. Then he dropped his clothes to the floor. His gun he replaced in its hiding place in the false bottom of the wardrobe drawer. With minimum waste of time, he used a rag and a bar of soap to give himself a sponge bath standing in the messy room. He found his remaining clean shirt on the floor, put back on the pants he had just removed and looked to see where the thugs had thrown his shoes. Though he peered under the bed, the wardrobe and the safe, he couldn't find them. Perplexed, he put on the shoes he had worn the day before, giving them a half-hearted buff with a piece of ticking.

The gold and ruby ring was still in his pocket, he found when he patted his hip to make sure. That would be his first move, he decided. Kumar, the jeweler, Marie and Glass had told him, worked from home in St James.

He brushed his hair and felt his cheeks and jaw line. There was some stubble but when people are trying to kill you for no reason, you don't take time to shave.

Opening the window a crack, he called Clarence again. "Boy," he whispered, when the child appeared, "I want you to watch this room for me today. If anybody come in, run to the station and tell Inspector McLeod one time. Nobody else." Clarence nodded. Clearly, he wasn't much of a talker. "And be careful. It have some dangerous men who looking for me. Don't talk to them if you see them. Just run for McLeod, alright?"

Clarence's grim nod was answer enough. Sonny shut the window and locked it. He put his long pewter key in the lock of the front door, after taking a close look at the street, but caught a glimpse of his room as he swung the door shut. Oh, what the hell, he thought, and left it unlocked.

CHAPTER TEN

It was not yet eight o'clock in the morning when Sonny got out of the westbound trolley at the turnaround near Harvard's Club in St James and walked to Nepal Street. The short street was a residential one but this was where Marie and Glass had assured him that he would find the jeweler he sought. Kumar's was a nondescript house of whitewashed tapia, with the obligatory front porch and a low hedge bounding the property. Without calling, Sonny boldly walked up to the front door. As he raised his hand to knock a fat woman in a pink sari opened the front door.

"Yes, may I help?" she asked. Her accent was as musical as her footsteps, which tinkled with a hundred tiny bells. She was a prosperous Indian lady, judging by the many gold and silver beras around her wrists. The bracelets, each as thick as a baby's finger, must have weighed a ton, Sonny thought.

"I am looking for Kumar."

She smiled, flashing as many gold teeth as stained brown ones. She nodded her head slightly and stepped aside, allowing him in to the cool, dim interior of the house.

"Where did you hear of us, may I ask?" she softly enquired, adjusting the feather light orni she wore around her neck and tucked into her waistband. The scarf covered just the bottom of her neck, letting her shiny black plait swing free down to her buttocks.

"Marie and Bobby Hackett."

Her smile nearly blinded him. "Such a lovely couple. We make for them many lovely things. And soon, another set of maljo beads, I think?" her smile grew mischievous as her cupped hands made a hump in the air over her corpulent belly. Sonny frowned. They hadn't said a word to him. But maybe Marie wasn't pregnant and this woman was mistaken. She continued, "We make the jet beads for bracelet for Jacob, when he born. And I try to get her to take one for herself. Baby not only one who get maljo; big people get bad eye, too. Jet and gold keep maljo away."

As she spoke she led him to the back of the house. In an airy, bright room was a man as round as she, bent over a table strewn with gold and gems. "Kumar, you have a customer. He is friends with Marie and Bobby."

Kumar, the less beautiful of the species, was as plain as his wife was adorned. He wore a simple white merino and black short pants. Leather slippers sat under his workbench; his feet were bare. Above his head a window let in the bright morning light.

"Morning, morning," he said, in an Indian accent thicker than his wife's.

"Morning." Sonny didn't waste a moment. This would be a long day and he wanted to get this over with. He handed the ring to its maker.

"Oh!" Kumar exclaimed, joyfully, sounding like a parent seeing a long-lost child. "Oh, I remember this!"

"Who is G.E.? And who is T.?" Sonny asked without preamble.

Kumar looked back up at his solemn visitor. "I am sorry. Who are you, friend of Bobby and Marie? And how you get this ring?"

Sonny sighed. "I'm a policeman." He didn't bother to add that he was on suspension. "I found the ring on a dead man who I think was a calypsonian named Jaguar. He was murdered yesterday and I have no idea why. I thought the ring would give me a clue to his life. You'd be surprised at how often a man is killed by the people who say they love him."

Kumar turned the ring around in his hand, looking at it through a loupe he extricated from the rubble of precious metals and stones on the bench. "I don't know. I don't know if I should tell you this. There are some things you don't tell strangers, even police." His fist curled around the ring. He looked at his wife, whose smile had dried up. All three of them looked grim as death.

"Tell him, beta. A man is dead," pleaded the woman, in her singsong voice.

Kumar opened his fist and looked down at the ring again. He held it up to the light. "See that?" he said to Sonny as the brilliant red stone flashed fire. "It is a perfect ruby. Perfect. I wish I could say I buy it but no, it was bring to me by a woman who say I make ring for her… for her friend."

He paused, looking wistfully at the stone again. It really appeared magical, blood red and clear, flawless and polished to mirror smoothness. "This stone," he said, "cost more than a policeman make in a year. Ruby not so expensive but this size, this perfect, it cost plenty, eh, beti?" he asked his wife with a little smile. She smiled back anxiously, bobbing her head. "So when a woman, who is not big aristo woman, when this woman bring this stone for me to make ring for her… friend, I say something not right.

"She say she get stone from she friend. And she show me papers. And papers in order but I still wait. I say Ganesh tell me when it alright to make this ring." At the sound of the name, Kumar turned and made a small gesture of obeisance to the murti of the elephant-headed Hindu god that had pride of place beside the window. The brass sculpture was about a foot high and wore a tiny garland around its neck.

"I wait and in one week she come back and say, don't bother, I don't have to make the ring. I give her back the stone and she go away.

"In two days she come back. This time she crying. She say I have to make the ring or she lose she work, she lil' popo, only two months, he go starve."

Kumar looked at his wife again. She was smiling sadly. "I take the stone. I make the ring. I write 'To G.E. Love T.' on inside, like she want. She never tell me who is these people. I just do what I do and she take the ring and she go."

Sonny exhaled slow and long. The jeweler had answered nothing with the story, only added even more complexity to the situation.

"But," Kumar's wife suddenly added, "you forget, husband, she give you address. She tell you her address."

Kumar was nodding, his eyes thoughtful. "Yes, true!" He turned to a deep biscuit tin at his feet under the workbench. It was full of slips of paper, some curling and discolored with age, others pristine and new. He rifled through the slips and with a soft cry of "aha!" pulled out one and handed it to Sonny.

The handwritten slip was a receipt for the ring. The writing was in an elegant script and made the bill out to Doreen Blackman. Her address was given as ten Gray Street, St Clair. At this, Sonny's eyebrows rose. "I thought you said she wasn't no aristo. This is an aristo address! Is only white people living there."

Kumar nodded. "White people and they maids."

Comprehension dawned. Of course, Sonny thought. After another moment studying the receipt, he had another question. "You said you saw a bill of purchase for the ruby. Did you copy the details?"

Kumar shook his head. "No, I did not. But I remember the name. I am not one of these bound coolies, you know," he added, suddenly. "Kumar Ragoobir come here a free man with a skill. I did not come here to cut cane like these indentured coolies. I come on HMS Hesperides to Guyana from Uttar Pradesh and I sail to Trinidad because they say is good living here. I learn English, I learn to read and to write in English since I am in India.

"I am a craftsman. My father, and his father, and my grandfather's father's father, we all make the jewels. All in India they know my family name for the jewels," he said proudly. Sonny was nonplussed but remained silent as Kumar continued. "The name on slip was James Harding." Sonny's eyes widened. "James Harding," Kumar repeated. "Was governor who buy stone."

What, Sonny puzzled, what on earth had he stumbled into when he jumped into the Dry River behind Clarence yesterday?

The body wore a ring that was set with a ruby owned by the island's governor, James Harding. But Harding wasn't the one who brought it to the jeweler. It was a ladies' maid named Doreen Blackman.

Doreen had given the address of a house twice as big as the one Sonny had grown up in. The Grande Riviere estate house his father had built was a rambling and lovely thing of cypre and white pine, with four bedrooms and two drawing rooms and a kitchen and a two-roomed annex for the maid and houseboy. The house on Gray Street dwarfed it. It was two stories high, for one thing, and from the outside seemed to have even more rooms on each floor than his sprawling childhood home.

Painted an austere charcoal, it was decorated with Baroque touches like a line of bas-relief cherubim on the lintels. Heavy red curtains hung in the windows, blocking Sonny's view of the inside of the house.

As he stepped on the pavement approaching the house, a slender Indian man carrying a rack of empty milk bottles came around the side of the building heading for the gate. Sonny waited until the man opened the gate before he said anything.

"Morning."

"Morning, sahib," the man said with a curious glance. "How you today. You want any milk?"

"No, thanks. But tell me, it have a Doreen working here?"

The man shook his head. He put down the rack of bottles and leaned on the wall, settling down for a chat. "That silly beti. Nah, she gone. They say they catch she thiefing some cheese in the pantry and send she home last week. Imagine," he said in a conspiratorial whisper, "these white people does buy ten bottle of milk from me a day. Them can't drink all that milk. And them can't eat half the food them have in there. But Doreen thief one little piece of cheese and is gone she gone." He sucked his teeth in disgust. As if the steups wasn't eloquent enough, he spat on the ground at his feet.

"You is friends with she?" Sonny asked.

"Yeah, we does friend," the porter said, turning the question around. "I like them creole girl. All that bumsee," he said, grinning and holding his hands wide to show how much bumsee he liked. "We start friending and we make a baby. A nice lil' boy. I going by them just now." He looked up. "How you know she? You is she family? I never hear she say she had no brother but you kind of favor she a little bit."

"No, I's not she brother."

The other man tensed. "Listen, partner, I don't want no trouble. We does friend but I is not she man. She say she ain't want no coolie man. If you is she man, I—"

"Nah! Nothing like that. I trying to find she to ask she about something," Sonny reassured the man. The man relaxed a little bit, still watching Sonny warily. "How you name?" Sonny asked. "I's Sonny Stone."

"They does call me Boyie, but my real name is Harinarine Lalbeharrysingh," the man said.

Sonny took the easy way out. "Boyie, nice to meet you." They grinned.

One of the heavy drapes on the second floor fluttered, a feat for something that must have been fifty pounds dry. The small movement drew Sonny's attention. He kept talking to Boyie but kept his gaze on the window. Soon enough, a white woman with a short blonde bob peered out at the two men talking on the pavement. Though the curtain dropped back into place a moment later, Sonny recognized the face instantly. Even from a distance.

It was hard not to. It was the face of Lady Albertina Harding, the governor's wife.

CHAPTER ELEVEN

Boyie's amiable grin was contagious. He brushed his perpetual cowlick from his left eye and bent to pick up the rack of empty milk bottles he had brought out of the Gray Street mansion.

Throwing a last glance at the imposing dark house, Sonny grinned back at his new friend. The pair walked towards the pastures a few blocks to the north where Boyie had tethered his two plump cows. This was his last delivery for the day and he had planned to visit his sometime girlfriend Doreen afterwards, he told Sonny, hinting strongly that he wasn't averse to being waylaid by some rum and old talk.

Sonny turned the idea over for only a second before he agreed to buy the cheerful Indian milkman a drink. Tim's would be open by the time they walked back from the pasture to Tragarete Road, a stroll of some twenty minutes if they kept their current pace.

The sun was already singeing the top of Sonny's unprotected head. He briefly regretted that he didn't wear hats, as one would have been sheer heaven in this heat.

Boyie was making small talk with the tall policeman when he said without warning, "What it is you really want with Doreen, boss? I know you say you is not she family and you is not she man. What other business you have with she, then? I ain't playing fast but is my child mother and I have to look out for she, you know?"

Sonny respected the younger man's bluntness. He didn't hesitate to roll out the whole story for him, down to his being attacked the night before. The only thing he left out was the part about him, Sonny, being a police constable.

"Perro?" Boyie's eyes widened and he let out a low whistle. "That is one nasty man."

"You know him?" Sonny asked quickly.

"Yeah. I did borrow some money from a man a time and he sell the paper to Perro. That bitch nearly break my hand when he come to 'talk' to me about why I ain't pay he back on time." Boyie shook his head slowly. "Bad news, man. Perro is not somebody you want to mix up with."

They walked in silence until they reached the pasture, Sonny again wondering where the trail of this dead man would lead.

Sweet talking his cows and affectionately rubbing their heads, Boyie pronounced them fine until he could return that afternoon. He hid his rack of bottles behind a bush and the two men turned back and set off for the Tragarete Road bar.

"So you feel Doreen go know who it is the ring was from? Them white people doesn't tell they maids nothing. Is just,

'Do this, do that.' They doesn't feel like we have feelings. I feel all white people wicked," Boyie said with anger. "Them bring we Indians here from cross the Kala Pani, promise we all kind of thing, and then leave we ass right here with we hand swinging. My father dead up inside of Bournes Road, right there in St James, so far, far, far from where he did born in India, and the last thing he did talking about was how them white people tell he they go send he back home."

Sonny reflected on Boyie's bitter words. It was something he had hardly considered. Growing up as he did surrounded by Africans, Indians and mixed race Venezuelans, he had come to consider all people the same, all blessed and cursed with human nature. And his first real contact with a white man had been favorable; Inspector McLeod, though his superior at work, had been an unquestionably honorable and fair man in all his doings.

"I don't know, nah, Boyie," Sonny said, looking at the road ahead. "It have bad white people. But it have good ones, just like it have bad black people and bad Indian people. Creole and coolie ain't have no better nature than anybody else. If somebody make you a god over a place and everybody in it, it must be hard to behave like you is a human," Sonny said.

"Where you from?" Boyie asked.

"Grande Riviere. You ever hear about there?" Sonny asked, grinning. It was a village so far up on the northeast coast of the island that few people knew of it at all. To call it a village was a generous term; it was a tiny collection of huts and shacks belonging to the people who worked the cocoa in the estate. A small dry goods shop there, run by a Portuguese trader, had folded for lack of business after only a few years. Not surprisingly Boyie had never heard of it.

"Is real far. You hear about Sangre Grande? Well, you pass there and you keep going. Is real far," he repeated. "But is like heaven. The place always green. You know how, when dry season come, it does get brown and dry? And the hills does catch fire because it so hot?" The withered grass all around them was a living testimony to what Sonny said. "Well, not in Grande Riviere. Is a forest, and it always have rain. Every day, it does rain and wet up the trees and the grass and the cocoa and make everything green, green. And you never drink water so sweet like what does run out of the spring in the hills. That water have a flavor. I feel it must be like what they does drink in heaven."

"Boy, if it so sweet, what the ass you doing in town?"

Sonny laughed at his new friend's refreshing candor. "It nice but it have nothing. In some ways it have everything but in other ways it have nothing. You can't go to school there, you can't get a work there, except in the cocoa, you can't meet a woman who you didn't know your whole life and see bathing in the spring in she bloomers twenty times already. You can't go nowhere. You can't do nothing.

"Man, I was twenty-one before I leave there to come and live in town. I never chase woman before. I never drink so much rum. I never meet so much of different people. I is not a real friendly fellow, I does more keep by myself. But I make some good friends here."

Boyie seemed to understand what Sonny meant. "So what work you does do?" he asked.

"I is a police."

Boyie stopped so suddenly he seemed likely to tip over. "So that is why you looking for she!"

"No, I done tell you why," Sonny said. "I on suspension. I only want to find she because, well…" he paused to find the right words. "One reason I leave Grande Riviere was because I love to find out things. Not from books and thing. I never like school so my mother never really push me to go. But I love to find out why things does happen, how they does work.

I feel like everything in life is a puzzle and you just have to watch it the right way to put the puzzle pieces together.

"Like I go watch you, for instance, and know that you must be meet Doreen when she was doing maid work by them white people and you try a thing plenty time before you get through." Boyie's rueful chuckle was answer enough. "And the only reason she must be let you get a little thing is because she just get fed up of you begging she every time you see she.

"But you love she bad, and she don't want you to married with she because you is a Indian."

"Sonny, how you know all that?" Boyie asked in wonder.

"Well, is partly things you say, partly just thinking, and partly knowing the place we living in and how people does act. I wrong?"

"No, no. You right. Except I never ask she to married. I know she go never do that. But in the meantime I taking what I could get and I giving what I could give. I real love she, too. And the little popo too nice. A little boy. If you see how he pretty. He have soft hair and dimples. I did wanted was to call he Krishna but she say she want to call he Christopher. So we just call he Chris and done the talk." He chuckled again. "One of these days maybe we go make a little girl to go with he. We real practicing, I go tell you that!"

The two men's laughter rang out in the mid-morning sunshine.

CHAPTER TWELVE

Dulcie, the wife and surly barmaid of Tim See Sing, was cooking up one of her rare and exceptionally tasty pots of pelau when Boyie and Sonny walked in to her husband's bar. She dished out the steaming plates of browned rice cooked with fresh pigeon peas and chicken, the creamy coconut milk in which it was boiled making it glisten.

As they ate, washing the food down with glasses of rum and water, the two men were silent. Sonny, for his part, couldn't get the mysterious ring out of his head. He still didn't know who was G.E., who was T., or what was the connection between the governor and his wife with this dead calypsonian. And how had the vicious Perro come into the picture?

The men caught a trolley bus to the city from the turnaround, on Sonny, emerging at the railway station on South Quay and walking the few blocks to Besson Street. Boyie had suggested they go there before visiting Doreen, to find out what McLeod had learned from Constable Evers' trip to Piccadilly Street the previous afternoon.

Evers, as surly as before, muttered under his breath about dirty coolies when Sonny and Boyie walked in. "Man, leave he, nah," Boyie said to Sonny when the latter bristled and made a move in Evers' direction. "I see what you mean. He is a creole and he treat me just like them white people." Boyie returned Evers' contemptuous look with interest, as he sat in the lobby waiting for Sonny to wrap up his business.

McLeod was excited to see his former constable. "Good God, man! Where have you been? I sent a runner to your house twice today and each time he came back empty handed. We have lots to do!" he said, before Sonny could respond. "Dead man's name was Glen Easton. He was in fact your calypsonian. Lived not on Piccadilly but on Prince Street. His sister Lucille lived with him. She identified the body this morning.

"Damnedest thing I ever saw. She refused at first, said she didn't have a brother. Then when the neighbor confirmed that she was the man's sister, she caved in. Claimed that her brother had no enemies except for rival calypsonians."

Sonny interrupted McLeod to ask if a skinny little boy had come to see him that day.

"No. Why? Did you send a message?"

"I was hoping he didn't," Sonny confessed, revealing the events of the previous night to McLeod.

"Yes, I have heard of Perro. Awful character, that one. We haven't got him pinned yet but we know he's got his hand in every filthy pie in this city. Fairly suddenly, too. Came out of nowhere, just after you got suspended, actually. We think he brings in babash from the country, sells it to the wangs. And he's also been suspected of being involved in whe whe. Then there's the prostitution and the moneylending. Damned frustrating, I tell you, not having any proof but knowing he's dirty."

Sonny knew what the old man was feeling. "Where are his headquarters?"

"Works out of the lodge on St Vincent Street. Well protected, I don't have to tell you that," McLeod added.

"The lodge" was a much-storied secret society of Freemasons. The group, all men of means, met under cover of darkness and were rumored to do demonic rituals to buy earthly success. Though he himself dismissed the talk of demons and Faustian deals with the devil, Sonny did have a firm belief in the evil that men do. He also knew that a man who had plenty to lose would not only watch his own back, but that of his friend as well.

"'Perro' is a pseudonym, I presume?" Sonny asked.

"Real name is Antonio Portallis. Venezuelan. His men call him Perro because he once bit a man's throat out, so the story goes."

Doreen, Boyie's son's mother, lived in Belmont. The narrow streets of the east Port of Spain suburb contained a mixture of middle- and working-class homes. Doreen lived in a working-class one, a board hut greying with age. The warped timbers were so far apart she had stuffed the gaps with newspaper, Sonny could see even from the street as he approached the rickety structure.

"I trying to get she to move up by me, but she ain't want to go," Boyie admitted, as they walked to the door. "Aye, girl!" he called, knocking on the front door. "Look I bring somebody who was looking for you!"

A sleepy-looking black woman opened the door. She was, to Sonny's surprise, nearly as tall and as dark as he. She and Boyie made a handsome couple, he lanky and fair, with wavy black hair falling over his fine-featured face, she lightly muscular, with short, kinky hair she had braided into fine plaits. Her face was smooth-skinned and her slanting, coal black eyes competed with her pink, pouting lips to be her best features.

Boyie introduced them and she let them in. The one-room shack was divided into two by a cotton sheet hung on a line across the middle. A long-limbed baby lay on the floor on a neatly folded bed of rags set back from the door.

"And I tell you he pretty?" Boyie whispered in delight at seeing his sleeping son.

"Come, let we go in the back. Mammy go watch he for me," Doreen said, leading them back outside to a bench propped against the back wall of the house. There they sat and Sonny again told his tale. He was getting heartily sick of it.

She shook her head when he came to the end.

"Mister, I don't know. The Ambroses and them is friends with the governor. I ain't going and talk to nobody about their business. Next thing I get lick up. What go happen to Chris if somebody do me something?" Her gaze was worried.

Boyie took her hand. "Girl, I ain't go let nothing happen to you. And why you protecting them white people? What they ever do for you? Not one fart."

Sonny said nothing. He knew she had a good point. It was all well and good for him to want to find out the truth but should she be a casualty of what was fast becoming a dirty war, what would become of Chris? The curly-haired infant sleeping inside the house would become a motherless child. And there was nothing sadder.

But what about justice? What about Glen Easton, a man who had met his end in a stinking dribble of water, his blood pumping out fast and hot towards the Gulf of Paria? What about him?

Making up his mind, he jumped to his feet and held out a hand to his new friend.

Boyie stood, shaking Sonny's hand.

"Good luck. Don't give up," Sonny added with a grin.

"So just so you gone?" he complained. "What about the ring? What about the puzzle?"

Sonny's smile slipped. "Something go work out." He tipped an imaginary hat to Doreen, who was biting her nails and looking agitated. "Miss Blackman." He spun on his heel and made for the street.

"Wait!" she said.

The word halted him in mid-stride. He came back, walking through the swept dirt of her yard and absently thinking that his shoes would absolutely never recover from the past two days.

"Is Tina. The name is Tina."

He furrowed his brow. Yet another to add to the meaningless stew of names in the mystery. Biting her lip and squeezing her eyes shut, the former ladies' maid exhaled on a sigh.

"Short for Albertina."

Boyie let out a whistle. "What! That calypsonian was friending with the governor wife!"

Sonny's stomach lurched. It was what he had feared. "Tell me what you know," he said to Doreen.

She looked fearfully at Boyie, who gave her an encouraging nod. Starting slow and soft, her voice gained strength as she went on with the story.

"I working for the Ambrose family for—" she turned to Boyie for confirmation, frowning as she did the simple sum— "about five years now? I is twenty now and I did start there when I did fifteen. So five years. I was in the kitchen first and then Missus Ambrose take a liking to me and make me she personal maid.

"It was nice, I get to do all the fancy hairstyles for she, with that pretty, straight hair and thing. I get real good at it, too. And then she tell she friends how I is a good hairdresser and they start to come over for me to do up their hair, too. One time," she said, with a tiny smile, "I did do six head of hair in one night. That was the night of the governor's ball.

"That was the first night I meet Miss Tina. She say to call she that. That she hate for people to call she Lady Albertina, how it sound like a old, fat cow."

"Is true," Boyie said, with a scoffing sound, "I had a cow name Albertina for true. One lazy bitch. I sell she."

"Anyhow, this fancy white woman, Miss Tina, start telling me all she business. And one day she tell me how she fall in love. How she fall in love with a nigger man."

CHAPTER THIRTEEN

Now that she had begun to tell the story, Doreen's fear seemed to evaporate, replaced by what Sonny would have sworn was relief. It made sense, in a way, he thought. Carrying that kind of secret around for any length of time would make a person's heart heavy. He remembered when he had first tried to keep a secret from his mother. Some little boy's crime, a broken bottle of perfume, or some spilt dusting powder, but it had eaten away at him from the inside until he couldn't look anyone in the eye. Now, he imagined that Doreen—who had done nothing wrong but couldn't tell anyone about the wrong someone else was doing—well, he imagined her burden was great.

"When was this?" he asked her.

"About eight months now? I did just make Chris. Like I say, Missus Ambrose did like me so when I make the baby she let me come back and work for she, even though I had was to go home for the two weeks. I know plenty people who does frighten to tell they boss lady how they pregnant, because they does want to fire you and doesn't want to take you back when you make the baby. But Missus Ambrose keep me, she let me work right up to when I take in with pains, and then once I take my nine-days' bath and come back, she even give me a band for my belly."

The ways of women were a deeper mystery to Sonny than even this murder. He only vaguely understood that Doreen meant she had had a bath steeped in medicinal herbs nine days after giving birth to Chris, and had been given a thick canvas strap by Mrs. Ambrose to hold in her slack abdominal muscles after the birth. If he had understood, it may have partly explained to him why she had a figure like a fresh virgin, despite the sleeping bundle of joy just inside her house.

"And even though I had was to leave Chris with my mother for most of the time, because I couldn't bring him to the house with me, I was glad for the little end. I was on my foot most of the time, yes, and listening to all them white women talk shit about they clothes and they man and they children and they parties—well, it was boring and I used to get vex how they had so much and they still wasn't happy. But is a work. And I rather do that than whore on George Street."

A short, groaning wail came from in the house. She stopped talking and cocked her head. The crying stopped. After a moment, she went on with her story.

"Miss Tina was the worst of all. Imagine you is a important lady like that, have all that money. Your husband is the governor of the whole island. Not just a Mr. Somebody here, like Mr. Ambrose. She husband is somebody in the world, important enough for they to give he a whole island to run for them. And she still taking man on the side." She steupsed.

"It just mad. That is what it is. Madness."

"So she was sleeping with this calypsonian?" Sonny asked.

"I ain't think they was sleeping, nah!" Doreen joked. "The amount of prick she say he was giving she, I doubt they ever sleep once. A time, she say them do it so much she nanny get sore and she had was to tell she husband how she get she monthlies twice for the month."

Governor Harding was probably not the smartest man in the world if he had fallen for that, Sonny thought. "But how they meet? And where they used to have they rendezvous?" At her puzzled look, he clarified. "Where they used to go and screw?"

"She meet he first time at the same ball. The governor's ball. All the fancy white people went, and even some aristo black people, too. I hear Miss Tina and Missus Ambrose talking about it afterwards. And Miss Tina tell me the story.

"He was the most handsome man she did ever see, she say. Tall and strong, with curly hair and nice, white teeth. And he used to smell like the sun, she say. I ask she what the sun smell like but she only grin. 'Like Glen!' she say. And he was a real cocksman—either that or she husband had a small, small thing. Because the first time that man give she some prick I didn't done hearing about it for months."

Doreen's eyes glazed over as she talked, not seeing the stand of citrus trees that separated her narrow back yard from her neighbor's. A bee buzzed around in the dark, shiny leaves of the trees, settling here and there until it flew off to more fulfilling endeavors. The trees were without flowers.

She continued. "He was singing at the ball when she meet him. He was so poor he couldn't afford pants for the fancy suit jacket the white people lend he, and he sing standing up behind a bar that block from he waist down. Underneath that he was in a dutty old pants. But she say he sing like a angel.

Me never hear no angel sing so, but you know how when you in love you doesn't see what really there?"

Sonny knew all too well about that. Witness: Joan.

"I in love with you and I know you can't sing," Boyie interjected.

"Boyie, hush your mouth and let me tell the story, nah," she scolded him. Sonny heard the words but also heard the caressing tone behind them. She may not have been able to say it, but the woman was in love with the lanky, pretty milkman. She had already seen beyond her prejudices; she only had to see that she had done so.

"She whisper to him to meet she in the bathroom and that is how it start. The first thing she do is buy a set of clothes for he."

Sonny remembered the sharkskin suit.

"And what she ain't buy, she forget. She used to give he money, gold, clothes, food, even a guitar. And everything she buy for him, she come back and tell me.

"The onliest thing she wanted was to buy for he again was a wedding ring. But of course, the lady did done married already. So she do the next best thing. She give he a ring and tell he how he can't screw with nobody else but she."

"That is the ring what you get Kumar to make for he?" Sonny asked, knowing the answer.

"Yes. She bring this big, dutty red stone, a ruby, and tell me to carry it by the best jeweler in the country and make it into a ring for she man. I didn't want to do it at first. The last thing I want to do is get tie up in these white people business.

"But she say… She say if I don't go, she go tell Missus Ambrose how I screwing with she husband."

Boyie, who had been listening with his eyes closed, jumped up. "What!" Doreen bowed her head. Both Sonny and Boyie knew then that the woman's threat had been based on fact.

"Not since I with you, Boyie," Doreen said, her voice low and sad once more. "I there since I is fifteen, I tell you. When I did first start working there, everybody tell me how I had was to be careful of the mister. But nobody didn't tell me he would have force heself on me. After the first time it wasn't so bad. By the time I reach eighteen he get fed up, and it had other, younger girls there by then. I was too old for he."

She looked up. "Boyie, I never went with he after I went with you. God is my witness."

The younger man was turning red with fury. His lips were a white line in his tan face. Doreen reached out a hand and stroked his set jaw. Sonny looked away, ashamed to see such a private moment and sorry that he had, in a way, precipitated it. When he looked back, Boyie was smiling slightly and Doreen looked calm.

"Well, I ask Boyie if he know any jeweler and he tell me about Kumar and I went and I take the ruby and I tell Kumar to make a ring for my friend. I figure she man hand couldn't be bigger than mines—" in truth, her hands were big, with thick, knobby fingers— "so to use my finger as the measure.

"But then Miss Tina come back and tell me don't bother, to go and take back the stone from Kumar. I feel she and the sweetman must be have a falling out and she want to break up with he. If that was true, then they must be make up again. Because after I did bring back the ruby, she send me back again. I tell she no at first but she threaten me again. I had was to do it.

"When I go back, something come on me and I get a feeling Kumar didn't want to make the ring at all. And I know she would have blame me if he didn't make it. I start to cry and tell Kumar how I go lose my work, and I tell he about the baby, about little Krishna," she said, with a small smile at Boyie, "and he agree to make the ring. "When I give she, Miss Tina say it was perfect. And I keep my work and everything was good. And she was so in love with she man and she husband getting horn and he didn't know nothing. Until Carnival come and that damn ass had to go and sing a song and tell every Tom, Dick and Harry how he was screwing the governor wife."

Sonny was confused, not by the tale but by the motives of a sweetman who would go out of his way to ruin what was essentially the best meal ticket he would ever find. A gigolo would have to be discrete, or he would run the risk of losing his livelihood. "What happen then?" Sonny asked.

"She husband nearly kill she. The next time I see she, she had a big blue mark on she hand, up here by she shoulder, and she was walking funny, like she foot break up. She stop talking to me. Last week Missus Ambrose say how she find a piece of cheese in my bag and how I had was to go home."

"Neemakharam bitches. White people too dutty and ungrateful," Boyie fumed.

Five years down the drain. Raped, taken advantage of, used and discarded. Sonny took Boyie's point about white people—these ones, at least. Wicked and bad.

CHAPTER FOURTEEN

"You never tell me where they used to meet," he asked Doreen.

She shook her head. "That is one thing I don't know. She never tell me exactly where, but she say it was by some fellow she know, not a white man, but another one of them colored aristos. She never tell me his name but she used to call him 'Old Dog'."

A shudder rippled through him when Sonny had heard the words. Perro, his mysterious nemesis, was pimping for the governor's wife. If she had held her secret assignations with the black calypsonian at Perro's house, there was no telling what influence the gangster wielded. It meant that if he wanted someone dead, they would die. Like Glen Easton a.k.a., The Mighty Jaguar. Like Sonny.

The question was why had Jaguar done what he had? To wreck a financially profitable—not to mention sexually thrilling—relationship with a wealthy white woman didn't seem like something a gigolo would do. Sonny knew that at least part of the answer lay with the dead man's sister. Her actions suggested that she knew more than she had let on to Inspector McLeod.

It was nearly five o'clock in the afternoon when he left Doreen and Boyie billing and cooing over their young son and made his way to the heart of the city. He wanted to talk to Jaguar's sister Lucille before nightfall. After which, Sonny thought, he wanted to be far away from Duke Street, Port of Spain, where Perro and his men knew to find him.

He didn't even have to look for Lucille. She was sitting on the step of an apartment on Prince Street between George and Charlotte. Sonny walked up to her boldly and came out with it at once.

"I know Perro had your brother killed. What I want to know is why."

Though her skin was the deep brown of aged cocoa beans, it grew pale when she heard the words. She shot to her feet and backed into the apartment, trying to close the door in his face. He stuck a foot in, once again rueing his ruined shoes as the door squeezed the once-flawless leather.

When Lucille realized she was no match for Sonny's strength, she relented. Wordlessly she opened the door and stepped aside. He walked inside.

The apartment was furnished exquisitely. There was a set of Morris chairs much like the one at Marie and Glass' home, a sideboard filled with glittering crystal and china, an ornately carved Indian screen, inlaid with ivory, separating the drawing room from the dining room. In the dining area, a tiny but perfect dinner table and four chairs reposed. Unlike Sonny's this was a two-room apartment. The second room was half-open; he could just glimpse a polished brass four-poster bed with a silken canopy. A chest of drawers, with a massive armoire to match, was crammed into the little bit of remaining space.

Lucille herself was in a stylish shirtwaist of pale silk. Her red patent leather flats proved her brother wasn't a selfish man, only a stupid one.

"Mister, I don't know nothing," she said. "That's rubbish," he dismissed. "He lived with you. You must know something. Anything."

"All I know," she said, with trembling lips, "is that my only brother get stab up by them sons of bitches and now he dead." Her eyes were full of water, which threatened to overflow.

"Look, I know who killed him. And all I want to know is why. Not why Perro killed him, but why Glen did something so foolish as to sing on the governor!"

Her stiff upper lip collapsed. Lucille began to sob. "I did tell he not to write that song! But he so harden, so harden. Since we small he harden. He say he ain't no bitch for she to tell he what to do, he is a man and he go do what he want."

So the song that had caused him to be killed was a boy's play for manhood? Sonny couldn't believe it and said so.

"Is true!" Lucille bawled into her cupped hands. "She buy all kind of thing for he. She buy he drawers and all. And he didn't want it but he take it. He say he love she and if that make she feel good he go take it. But is when she say she want to give he that blasted ring, and tell he how he is she own, then like he went mad.

"He cuss she black is white and tell she he is a man and you can't buy a man with a pissing tail ring. He leave she. But she beg back. She send all kind of message for he, begging for he to come back. That was months before Christmas but she send so much gift for he you would have think it was Christmas already." Her eyes still streaming tears, she abruptly stalked into the bedroom and flung open the wardrobe. It was jammed with suits, shirts, trousers, of all colors and descriptions. Only one tiny space was devoted to dresses. Glen's largesse was nothing to his lover's, it seemed.

"Look at that. She buy till she couldn't buy again. They didn't have nothing leave in the store! And he take it. But he heart was heavy. I tell he, 'Glen, don't write that song.' And when he write it anyway, I tell he, 'Glen, don't sing that song.' But he sing it, in Hell Yard, and in Big Bamboo Yard, and in any blasted yard that would let him sing. And he take she self money and make a record of the song, so now all over the world every bitch and he brother know my brother was screwing the governor wife.

"'*Ah me!*'" she began to sing.

"*You never see such a thing!*

As when the black cock beat the white cock in the ring!

Ah me! You never see such a thing!

As when the black cock beat the white cock in the ring!

The governor was a man who like fighting cock

He cock white and small but it had a loud squawk.

One day he wife bring another cock home

A fine black cock with a big cockscomb.

The white cock get in the ring and rear up

But the black cock beat him before a minute up.

You never see such a scandalous thing

The governor wife give the black cock everything."

Her voice was mellow and sweet, a female version of the one that had won Lady Albertina's heart. As she sang, Sonny began to understand why the man had done it. Albertina Harding had taken his manhood. Glen Easton had sung it back to life in grand style.

Sonny broke the silence following the song with a question. "What you know about Perro?"

"Only that he is bad news," she said, drying her eyes on a satin shirt from her brother's collection. "He used to drop all the gifts from she. And is by he they used to go and do they nastiness. Somewhere in Maraval. Real far, up in the bush."

Sonny smiled to himself. She had no idea what bush really was.

"But what is their connection?" He couldn't imagine the governor's wife metaphorically getting into bed with such a lowlife.

She shrugged. "Glen say he meet him at the governor's ball, the same night he meet she. That is all I know." She smiled crookedly. "Really, this time."

Dark was about twenty minutes away. He stealthily walked the few blocks to his home, looking around every couple of steps. Cautiously pushing in his door, he was once again shocked by his room's appearance. It was spotless.

And Vero, Clarence's mother, was sitting on his bed.

"Mister, who you is and what you getting my son involve in?" she demanded as he walked through the door.

He had only a few moments to spare, none of which he could spend talking to Vero. Ignoring her question, he grabbed a grip from the top of the press and started throwing things into it. Where *was* his other pair of shoes?

"Mister! I talking to you!"

Sonny straightened briefly. "Look, Vero. I sorry I get your boy involved. Or rather, I sorry your boy get me involved. He is the one who find the body in the first place. But now all of we go be in big trouble if dark catch me here. So I packing up and going. You could do what you want but I have to go. Right now." He returned to the press, withdrawing the two guns and their bullets from the secret part of the drawer. He crammed the rifle in the grip diagonally and stuck the loaded revolver into his waistband.

Vero blanched at the sight of the guns. "Who you is in truth?" She demanded again.

Sonny had finished packing up. "Is you who clean out for me?"

She nodded.

"Thanks. How much I have for you?"

Vero drew up her spine straight. "Nothing. I didn't do it for money."

"Have it your way," Sonny said, with a shrug. Vero watched as he turned to walk away, then put out a hard hand to stop him.

"You don't even want to know what happen to Clarence today? Them men and them come back. They beat him bad."

CHAPTER FIFTEEN

Robinson Edwards, Papa Phil, as he was known on the hill, opened his back door to Sonny and Vero without saying a word.

The house high on Rose Hill, Laventille, was the only place Sonny could think of that was safe from Perro. Though it was walking distance from the city, Papa Phil's house seemed like it was in another world. The long, narrow board house, in better shape than Doreen's had been, was tucked into a verdant cut of the highlands that towered over the city's eastern side. Reached by a dirt track off the steeply curving main road, the house was nearly invisible because of all the trees that surrounded it.

It was what Papa Phil needed. His job description required he be hard to find. Papa Phil was an obeah man.

He was also Sonny's former father-in-law.

Joan, the woman who Marie Hackett blamed for ruining Sonny's life, had been the most beautiful woman he'd ever seen. Blacker than him, with skin that felt as silky as a baby's, Joan stood just tall enough to fit in the curve under Sonny's arm when he held her. And he had held her a lot. The full curves of her body had sung to him in four different languages, all of them saying the same thing: "Come."

Joan had been plump, with chubby cheeks and laughing eyes and a bottom that Boyie, the creole-loving bumsee man, would have cheered lustily. It was as round as two over-sized mammy apples rolling in a bag. The forest fruit, tangy sweet and firm, was about the size of a large grapefruit; Joan's bottom was perhaps three times that and perfectly proportioned to the rest of her curves.

Sonny had loved her the day he met her three years before while walking on a foot patrol in Laventille. But she was training to be a teacher and at first wanted none of the gentle, quiet policeman. She had her sights set on being trained further than this island could offer, in spite of her ebony black skin and all it implied for her dreams. As hungry for book knowledge as Sonny was for human understanding, she whizzed through primary school at Morvant Anglican and won a full scholarship to the new Anglican girls' high school established by the bishop in St Ann's. She seemed just what they wanted, an enterprising black girl who wanted to rise above her history.

But while they wanted her to rise above it, Joan had her own ideas. She took their education but not their religion. While going to Anglican church on a Sunday, dutifully reciting the English prayers and singing the flat and somehow mournful hymns, she went secretly to her father's house when he had palais. Papa Phil was not only expert in roots, herbs and bush medicine, he had a spiritual role as head of the Shango church he ran in the dirt-floored chamber behind his house.

He was the one to see when you wanted to catch a man, to hold a woman, to make a baby or to throw one away. He wouldn't curse anybody, he always said, because what you do rebounds to you in one way or the other. But Sonny was willing to bet that he had the knowledge and the wherewithal to do so if pressed.

But it wasn't Papa Phil's spiritual assistance he needed tonight.

What Papa Phil saw when he looked out that night was Sonny holding a bulging grip in one hand and hoisting a bone-thin boy against his chest with the other. Standing at his side was a thin woman with skin the golden brown of a walnut shell, her head tied in a neat blue cloth, wearing a white shirtwaister of rough flour bag fabric.

Papa Phil asked nothing. He led them into the house, which smelled of incense and some bittersweet fragrance Sonny could not identify.

Dozens of framed prints of Renaissance paintings of Catholic saints hung on every wall. The house was clean and uncluttered. Simple wooden benches had been placed in a circle around a center table, all varnished terra cotta brown. A brass pot of red ixoras and croton leaves was on the middle of the little round tabletop. A buffet, holding few items, was against a far wall. A commemorative plate with His Majesty's face on it was propped proudly on top of the sideboard, which was the only store-bought piece of furniture in the house.

Sonny knew that in the next room there was a board bed and a table covered in candles, pictures of saints, incense sticks perpetually burning, and flowers of all kinds. A small dish of fruit would be put out, another of honey, yet another of corn, to appease the various deities the saints represented.

Shango took half its doxology straight from the Catholic church, using many of the same prayers and rituals as Rome; the central difference was that while Shangos prayed to Jesus as Lord, they also adhered to a polytheistic faith that venerated African orishas. The orishas, gods, took on the aspects of the Catholic saints. So Jesus was also Shango, god of lightning and the storm. Other saints were Legba, the god of iron, Eshu, the mischievous god of the crossroads, Yemanja, goddess of the rivers and oceans, and Oludumare, the father of the gods.

When he was leading his little church—which met infrequently these days—Papa Phil wore a white robe with a red cummerbund. Otherwise, he wore regular clothes. Tonight, he was in a shirt of indeterminate color, sheer with age, and brown short pants. He was a skilled carpenter as well as a medicine man. Sonny knew the old man had built the house and many of its furnishings himself.

"Sit down," invited Papa Phil after the introductions were made. "What happen to the boy?"

Sonny held the sleeping boy in his lap. Even in the shifting lamplight it was clear his face was swollen.

"He get beat up. Some bad men beat him up, Papa Phil. And is my fault." Sonny's voice was shadowed with grief. The frail body hitched a shallow breath, let out on a trembling sigh. The boy snuggled closer to Sonny's warmth.

Papa Phil took him up in his arms. It was no challenge. The stocky old man had a slight limp but Clarence weighed so little that it was hardly a strain to bear him. He took the sleeping boy into the bedroom and put him on the bed.

"You give him aloes?" he asked Vero, who nodded in response. "When he wake I go fix up something for he to drink. Don't worry, he go catch heself. He take some lash but I ain't feel nothing break."

Vero's eyes lost none of their fear. She knew that the clear, slimy, bitter flesh of the succulent aloe leaf, which she'd given the boy to swallow, would reduce the swelling and bruising. But there was more to her fear than just the physical.

Papa Phil turned to Sonny. "What this is about?"

Sonny unfolded the story for him without hesitation. The old man listened without comment. At the name Perro he lifted an eyebrow but still said nothing. When the last word was spoken, he nodded once and rose. "She could sleep with the boy. You and me go go outside."

Sonny threw an eye at Vero but she seemed locked in her pain and didn't see him. As Papa Phil passed her, he touched her shoulder. "Don't fret, sister. It is in His hands now and He never fails." Sonny followed the old man out the door and into the palais.

The cool dirt floor was smooth and silky. Sonny knew his ex-wife's father lepayed it with fresh cow dung, letting it dry to an even, odorless grey. The room was about twenty feet square and could hold only a few people at a time; Papa Phil had only a small flock.

They took off their shoes at the door and sat on benches facing each other.

"That Perro is a bitch. I ain't hear nothing good about he since I first hear he name. You watch yourself."

Sonny sighed. "Is not like I went looking for this. The boy find the body. What I was suppose to do? Just go home and forget I see it?"

"That might have be the better thing to do," Papa Phil said, chuckling. "But now you in it, let we win it!"

Sonny looked affectionately at the old Shango baba. He looked like his daughter, with her laughing eyes and round cheeks. They shared the same ebony skin. At the mental image of her, Sonny felt the same falling away in his belly he always felt when he thought of Joan. He looked away.

"What you going to do?" Papa Phil asked.

"I have to get him before he get me," Sonny said quietly.

"Careful you don't buy trouble. You can't carry it back, eh."

"Done in trouble already. Didn't buy it, I get it free. Might as well use it since I have it."

He outlined his plan to Papa Phil, who had one small change to suggest. The men talked until the single candle burning on the altar of the chapel was low and dim.

CHAPTER SIXTEEN

Soft footsteps on the wooden floor of Papa Phil's drawing room woke Sonny, who had slept there. Vero's feet, as thin and brown as the rest of her, were in front of his face.

He sat up, stretching. It had been a sound rest, better than he had had for months, despite the hardness of the floor. When he looked into Vero's face, they were both smiling.

"That man does work miracles!" she said, happiness ringing in her tone. "If you see Clarry! Like nothing at all happen."

"Where him?" Sonny asked, stretching his long limbs again.

"He climbing a tree and trying to give heself colic with young mango," she complained lovingly.

He noticed that she had not yet tied up her hair. It was lush and golden brown—what Sonny's mother used to call "sugar head"—naturally straight and reached halfway down her back.

Sonny, who had slept bareback in his trousers, got up and slipped on his shirt. Vero's eyes slid boldly down his hard, black chest. Sonny caught her eye. A red blush crept up her neck and suffused her light brown skin, but she didn't look away.

A shout from their host shattered the moment.

They walked outside to the little kitchen that annexed the house. Inside, Papa Phil was stirring a pot over a pitch oil stove. The kitchen was redolent of bay leaf and nutmeg.

"Morning. I hope you like cornmeal porridge," the old man said. "It have coffee if you want."

Sonny helped himself to the steaming coffee, which he poured from a pot through a strainer into an enamel cup. Vero accepted a smaller cup of the bitter, strong brew. Fresh milk and some sugar stirred into it made it just palatable. Papa Phil was no coffee maker.

Clarence's laughter rang out in the cool morning air. A tree in the yard close to the palais rustled. The spry boy leapt from a low branch to the ground and ran barefoot to the kitchen.

"Careful!" Vero admonished him with the beginning of an anxious look.

Papa Phil clucked at her. "You mustn't pet and pamper him so. He is a boy, nearly a man. He have to learn to stand up on he own two foot."

She bit her lip. Clarence rushed past her to hug Sonny

round the waist.

"Mister Sonny! Mister Sonny! I see a bird and some eggs in a nest! And the bird pick me but I touch the eggs—"

"Why you interfering with the—" Vero began, then hushed as Papa Phil threw her a glance.

"What kind of bird? You know?" Sonny asked.

"Well, I know is not a pigeon or a kiskidee," the boy said breathlessly. "But I only know two kind of bird so—"

The adults all laughed. Sonny ruffled his hair and promised he'd watch the nest to see what its tenants were.

At a simple pine table in Papa Phil's house they ate the porridge. It was rich and sweet, thick with fresh milk and flavored with honey and spices. He couldn't make coffee to save his life but Papa Phil knew his way around a porridge pot.

They didn't rush. Sonny had told them he would stay in hiding that day, intending to work out the details of his plan in the seclusion of the little house in the Laventille bush. Until Perro was dealt with, one way or the other, neither he nor Clarence would be safe in their homes on Duke Street.

"You hear from Joan?" her father asked.

Sonny shook his head. The mention of her name caused the falling away of the bottom of his stomach once more. Would he never get over her? It had been six months since he last saw her.

Then she had been dancing like a woman possessed. Which, in a way, she had been. Mounted by a spirit during a Shango meeting, she had caught the power and was dancing in service of her god. Sonny, his starched uniform itchy in the muggy heat of that November night, had burst into the palais—not the one behind Papa Phil's house but another, deeper in the bush, led by a woman known as Mother Mary— with five other constables and Sergeant Sandy.

As hard as he had tried to get out of going on the raid, it was his job to squelch the Shango church. The Shouter Baptist Ordinance made the church illegal. Constable Johnson Stone was after all a member of Her Majesty's police force in Trinidad.

Bull pizzles swinging, the police backed the church members into a corner and began to arrest them. Though the Shangos outnumbered the officers three to one, few struggled. But when they were brought out of the church, more than one made a break for the thick bush. Joan, her eyes still glazed, was one of them.

Sonny let her run. Sergeant Sandy shouted to him, "Look she getting away! Hold she!" But Sonny wouldn't hold her. He stood with his hands limp at his sides and watched his new wife bolt into the dark night.

He was suspended the next day and got divorce papers the next week.

It was the beginning of his six months in hell.

Joan never communicated with him or tried to see him. Peters, his lawyer, handled the divorce quietly and swiftly, telling Sonny when he inquired that Mrs. Stone wanted nothing from their two-month marriage, not even the wedding ring. She had returned it in an envelope. The next Sonny heard was that she had sailed for England. She never wrote.

The Duke Street apartment seemed bigger than it had before she had brought her laughter to it. She had kept insisting, during their short marriage, that he needed more furniture. Now he didn't.

He hated to play the game of "if only" but in the dim silence of his room he played it every day. If only he had told her that he was going on a raid. If only she had been honest with him and told him she was going not to her father's house but to the palais up the hill. If only she had told him she was back in the Shango faith. If only she hadn't left Trinidad. If only he had been man enough to find her. If only. If only.

"Sonny, it wasn't suppose to be," Papa Phil's gruff voice broke into his thoughts. He was the only person who knew the whole story. Sonny had come to him, wild with fear, looking for Joan after the raid but Joan had been there before him. Been and gone. The old man not only knew the whole story, he knew both sides of it.

"She is my child so I could tell you she never love you like she should have. She was not the woman for you."

Vero sipped her porridge and kept her eyes looking down at the table. Whatever these men were discussing had nothing to do with her. She would do her best to pretend that she wasn't there. Clarence opened his mouth to ask who they were talking about but she silenced him with a swift cut eye. He too bent his head and concentrated on his breakfast.

"She did always like the church," Papa Phil mused. "I wasn't sure she would have be a iya. Her mammy wasn't interested in that at all, and being a church mother is a big risk, a big responsibility.

"And you know, she did try to leave it. But when the spirit call you, you have to answer. It wasn't Joan who you try to lock up, it was Oshun. And Mother Oshun is not a goddess to tamper with. She sweet but she strong. And she vindictive. Joan couldn't go back to you after what you do. Oshun wouldn't have let she."

Sonny drank his cornmeal porridge down and stood without comment. Taking the earthenware bowl out to the yard he washed it in water dipped from a big copper hemisphere half-sunk into the ground. It was a relic from some nearby sugar plantation. Once used for boiling cane juice to make sugar, it now served as a receptacle for water.

Papa Phil, like most of the hill's residents, depended on rainwater for his daily needs, but during the dry season when rain hardly fell he had to walk down the hill to the standpipe to fetch water by the bucket. It was tedious and strenuous, especially for Papa Phil with his limp, but since he didn't own his land and wasn't a property tax payer, the colonial government didn't see it fit to provide water to his home. In fact, relatively few of Laventille's residents were bona fide. The hill was largely a community of squatters, whose parents and grandparents had claimed crown lands there after Emancipation eighty-four years before. Mostly African, the population had been swelled slightly by indentured Indians who came looking for a chance outside of the cane when their contracts ended.

Because Laventille was mostly poor and black and Indian, the colonial government had little use for it. Fair enough, the people seemed to say; they had little use for the government. They feared and hated the police, the government's enforcement arm, and took every chance to flout the force's authority. And that included in matters of religion. Shango, the banned faith, thrived there, partly because of the strong African community, partly in defiance of the police's authority. The Ordinance was blatantly racist, anyway. It was put in place to suppress one of the few things black Trinidadians had that was their own. Unlike Indians, enslaved Africans weren't allowed to keep their native names, though they survived in bastardized forms through and after the four-hundred-year ordeal of slavery. They weren't allowed political or economic power, and weren't as a class land or property owners— although there were exceptions, such as Sonny's own clan. Everything was designed to make them feel ashamed of their color and race. The name Africa had become almost a curse, although in England and Jamaica some black people were beginning to fight against it with movements to reclaim the motherland as their own.

Shango was a distorted memory of the faith of their fathers. They were pressed into Catholic, Anglican and Methodist churches during slavery, threatened with death if they practiced their native religions. But the old gods were wily. Instead of disappearing they changed their shapes, hiding in plain sight.

Sonny was damned if he was going to fight with the white colonial government to take that memory of Africa away from them.

That was why, time after time, he refused to tell the commissioner of police that he had made a mistake in letting the Shango woman go. The commissioner had had no idea that Joan was Sonny's wife. He had long kept his private life and his job separate. Perhaps too well.

CHAPTER SEVENTEEN

Unsure where Perro's house was, Sonny left Rose Hill before dawn the next day, carrying a long canvas sack on his back. He headed to Belmont, where he was sure he would find his newfound friend Boyie. Sure enough, the Indian milkman was pulling up his trousers and walking away from the board outhouse behind Doreen's hut when Sonny came by.

Though they had known each other less than two days, something in the younger man's manner made Sonny sure he would be useful in a jam. Under Boyie's playful exterior there was a well of bitterness Sonny had glimpsed. That could be turned into something more productive. Anger without focus was just wasted energy; put to use, it could be deadly.

He sketched out the details of his plan.

"Only problem is I don't know where he living," Sonny grumbled.

"Yeah," Boyie muttered. "I wish I could have tell you but I don't know myself. But Maraval is a small place. One small village, a church and then some people up a steep, steep hill. But mostly just coffee and forest."

Sonny knew it could be suicide, but he planned to raid the home of his unseen nemesis Perro. The village, though small, did have a police station. Sonny thought his best bet for finding out the location of Perro's house was to take the direct route and ask at the station. Boyie had a better idea.

"Big man like that, he bound to have a motor car. Can't have too many of them in Maraval. Let we just look for the motor car and we go find the man."

Leaving Sonny's bag behind, they rode the train as far as it would take them and hitched a ride on a donkey cart the rest of the way. Sonny had worn his one jacket, simply to conceal the blue steel revolver hidden in his waistband. He and Boyie made an odd couple, the lanky Indian dressed in stained khaki pants and a dirty white merino and the massive black man dressed in a suit. But fashion wasn't high on either man's list of priorities. They had murder on their minds.

The village was as small as Boyie had said. A church on a little rise, a Catholic primary school, a police station, one or two shops and houses. The rest was hidden in rolling green hills. The carter dropped them off just before the church. They headed for the police station.

A bored-looking constable was smoking a cigarette at the station door. He looked like he had been in a fight; one side of his face was puffy and he held his arm at a funny angle when he put the cigarette to his lips. Sonny took a closer glance at the rest of the man. What he saw took him aback. There on the constable's feet were the patent leather shoes the thugs had stolen from Sonny's apartment.

Sonny grabbed Boyie's shoulder and pulled him back in a rough hug, redirecting him to the road leading up the hill opposite the church.

"Don't say nothing, just walk like you was always going up the hill," Sonny said in a low voice. Boyie nodded and smiled. When they were far enough from the station that Sonny was sure the constable could no longer see them, he explained to Boyie what had happened.

"So that mean—"

"So that mean Perro have the police involve in this too. I should have know. This stink going all the way to the governor house."

Boyie's hunch about the car proved right. A gleaming maroon Model T roared on the road around the bend behind them. Hearing the motor the men dived for the bush, hiding just in time to see it pass. A wavy-haired black man in his thirties, so light he could pass for white if he hadn't had a broad nose and thick lips, sat in the back seat flicking through a newspaper. Sonny recognized the driver. It was the same stammering boy who had attacked him at his apartment two nights before. Sonny hoped he didn't have to follow through on his threat.

When the car was out of sight, the men crept from the bushes and walked in the same direction. Soon enough they came to a sprawling, white, wooden house at the end of a short driveway. The maroon car was parked beside the house.

Now they had found their target, Sonny and Boyie turned around and went back the way they had come.

Back in Port of Spain, Sonny sought his solicitor's office on Abercromby Street. James Peters, an old mulatto who had served Sonny's father before him, was overjoyed at the news that the Hacketts were finally buying the Roberts Street cottage. The price Sonny suggested was several thousand pounds below what Peters would have liked but his client was adamant and wouldn't be swayed. Peters sighed and made a note of the ridiculously low figure. He would get in touch with the couple within a few days, he told Sonny.

The young black constable had one more thing to discuss.

"I want to make up my will," Sonny told him.

"Capital idea, man," Peters grunted. "Beneficiaries? Executor? Well, me, of course," he said, with a little grin, showing yellowed teeth and blackened gums. Sonny was glad he didn't count cigarettes among his vices. Women and rum were bad enough.

"Give half of it to Marie and Bobby Hackett," he began. He remembered the jeweler's wife's speculative comments on Marie's possible pregnancy. "With a special grant of one thousand pounds to their son Jacob—and any other children they might have at the time of my death. Give one quarter to Harinarine Lalbeharrysingh, of Bournes Road, St James. And the remainder to be divided between Edward Robinson, of Rose Hill, Laventille, and Clarence Timothy, of fifteen Duke Street, Port of Spain.

"And yes," he added, "of course you'll be my executor."

The solicitor scribbled notes onto a sheet of paper on the desk in front of him. "Timothy, you say?" He scribbled some more. "I can get this to you by next week."

Sonny shook his head. "No good. I need it by today."

"Today!" the lawyer looked scandalized.

"Can't you just write it out now and I'll sign it? Your secretary can witness it."

Peters looked like he had bitten a lime. "Yes, I suppose so. Miss Morel!" A leggy young woman, as light-skinned as Peters himself, came in after a moment. "Take some dictation."

The secretary modestly perched on a chair, then ruined the effect by hitching up her slim skirt and crossing her legs at the knees. Sonny got an eyeful. She noticed and gave him a wink, too, as she licked a pencil's point and said, "Ready when you are, boss."

"Date, address. I, Johnson Stone, Junior, of fifteen Duke Street…"

By the time he left the lawyer's office an hour later, he had a copy of his will, signed and sealed, in his jacket. His next stop would be the Hackett's home in Woodbrook.

Glass was working in his shop, nearly hidden by a stack of clear glass as tall as he was. "Boy, like every window in Trinidad break yesterday," he grumbled to his old friend.

Sonny didn't tarry. He handed the will to Glass.

"What is this?"

"My will. Keep it safe until… well, just until," Sonny said. He wasn't smiling.

"Want to tell me what the ass going on?" Glass hadn't forgotten their conversation about the dead man but had no idea that Sonny had been attacked. Sonny caught him up to speed. All he could do was whistle. "That is something, man." He paused, the light of comprehension dawning in his eyes. "Don't tell me you going up there?"

Sonny said nothing.

"You is a madman? They go mash you up fine, fine!"

"Glass, I know that. But what kind of man go just sit down and wait for somebody to come for him? If this thing is as bad as I feel it is, if the governor really involve, then nowhere I go in Trinidad, nowhere I go in the whole Empire, I could rest. That is no life for a man."

Glass looked to argue. Sonny shut him up with a raised palm. "I going. You can't stop me."

The little man had not a moment's hesitation after that. "Then I going with you."

Sonny, with Glass in tow, met Boyie at dusk at the Queen's Park Savannah where the Saddle Road began. The sprawling green park, miles in circumference, was empty, its last late evening strollers having just gone. Sonny introduced his oldest friend to his newest one, and the three started walking up the twisting road to Maraval.

A rattling lorry slowed and stopped in front of them. "Allyuh boys want a drop?" a toothless old man offered from the driver's seat. The jalopy took them most of the way. They had about ten minutes' walk to get to the big, white, wooden house in the forest. Silently, the men split up. Sonny took the back door.

CHAPTER EIGHTEEN

The stammering boy was the first man down, felled in the back doorway under a swift punch from Sonny's elegant fist. Sonny itched to keep his promise to kill the boy but held back. There was other business at hand. Another guard, dozing lightly at the table in the dining room, was roughly awakened and immediately put back to sleep by Sonny's tender mercies.

Ruthlessly the tall, dark man stalked through the house on cat's feet, knocking out one more man before he found the object of his search, Perro, reading a book by lamplight in the drawing room.

Antonio Portillo didn't look surprised to see Sonny.

"Ah, Constable Stone! So pleased that you could join me," he mocked in perfect English, lightly accented with a Spanish inflection.

"What can I do for you?"

By this time Boyie and Glass had made their own way in. Boyie took up position by the front door, holding Sonny's rifle in hand. Glass guarded the other door to the drawing room, armed with a long and wickedly sharp cutlass. The curving machete blade was dull silver at its edge.

Sonny took out his revolver. "I didn't want it to come to this."

Portillo raised his eyebrows at the sight of the gun. "I never took you to be the kind of man who would take justice into his own hands, Constable. What about 'Vengeance is mine, sayeth the Lord; I will repay'?"

"I didn't notice the Lord doing anything when your thugs were trying to beat me up," Sonny replied dryly. "And when they beat up the little boy, I think He should have done something a little more… visible, don't you think?"

Portillo laughed, his fleshy lips stretched in apparent pleasure at Sonny's wit.

"You are a funny, funny gentleman, Constable. But this is no laughing matter, is it?"

"No," Sonny agreed. "You killed Glen Easton over a calypso. I think that's the bottom line. And we both know you'll never go to jail for it. Which is neither here nor there to me," Sonny heard himself saying. The words rang true, even though they were a surprise to him. Through the last ten years, the last six months, and especially the last three days, he had completely lost faith in the system of the colonial government. They would always protect their own. And Antonio Portillo was one of theirs, for good or ill.

"All I want to do is to make sure that you get off my back,"

Sonny added. "I thought I'd ask you nicely. First."

"Ah, Dios mio!" Portillo cried, chuckling. "So dramatic!" He still held the book in his hand. Calmly he marked the page and put it on a side table. "Tell me, Constable, do you have any brothers? No? Then you have no idea what this is all about. Glen, my little brother, the cocksman, the one with the flash and the flair. The one who could make any woman fall in love with him at the drop of a hat. He was going to ruin everything. He had to die."

Sonny was stumped. He had had no clue that the two men were related. "Lucille say she only had one brother."

"Lucille, pah," Portillo said, dismissively. "She is the baby. She knows nothing but what Glen told her. She was born here, unlike the two of us boys who were born down the Main. Mama was a Trinidadian. Papa fell in love with her but you know how some men love with their fists. She came over with Glen when he was a little bambino, leaving me with my papa. Papa came to see her once—and left her a little present, that was Lucille—but they were… how do you say it? Incompatible." He reached into his jacket. Sonny raised the gun and Portillo's hand slowed. "Just a cigarette. Do you mind?"

Lighting the cigarette, he continued. "I lived with my father, in Venezuela. He wasn't much of a businessman but he did all right. He saved much more than I knew, because he left me a tidy sum when he passed last year. When I came here to find my baby brother—yes, to give him his share, I am a fair man—I found that there were many opportunities for an enterprising businessman."

Opportunities like gambling, whoring and running illegal bush rum, Sonny thought.

"But a man is worth little unless he knows the right people. Money is fine—but influence! If you have that you can rule the world."

He took another deep draw on the cigarette. The night outside was quiet but Sonny could hear every chirping cricket, every piping frog. There was no breeze. It was a still night and the air was heavy.

"It was a simple idea. He would seduce the white woman and so gain her husband's ear. I would smooth the path for their young love. And if I picked up any useful friends along the way, well, so be it. Their rutting drove me out of my own house," he said with a grimace. "So loud. So frequent. But the spoilt boy ruined it all when he sang that foolish song.

"I told her to sue him for libel. But she said nobody sues a calypsonian, it just was not done. She insisted he had to die."

Sonny watched the heavy-faced mestizo with contempt. He could guess what was coming next.

"Influence. What is it worth? Is it worth a brother's life? I thought so. Imagine if I could do her this favor. I could be so close to the governor, it would be like having a seat at his dinner table."

He took another drag and dropped the burning cigarette butt to the floor. "And then you came along. You see," Portillo said, rising, "the only thing that linked me to that puta was Glen. And the only thing that linked Glen to her was that ring. Which I believe you still have." As he spoke he began walking towards Sonny. "I want it back."

Sonny held the gun up with a steady hand. Portillo ignored it and kept walking. Without warning he launched himself at Sonny, teeth bared.

One shot rang out. Portillo fell to the floor in a spreading pool of blood. The man looked surprised and a small smile tried to emerge from those thick lips. "She said her husband told her the ruby was bad luck. But she wasn't supersti—"

It was the last thing he ever said.

The three men looked at each other once more and left the building, heading home.

Sonny went back to Papa Phil's home on Rose Hill. He let himself into the house and lay on the floor, falling asleep as his head hit the wood. Sometime later, when it was still dark outside, he felt a mouth on his. Thin hands held his face. He didn't say anything. Sometimes there are words for things and sometimes there aren't.

"Papa Phil," he asked the following day, "it have such a thing as bad luck?"

The old obeah man considered the question. "Huh. Well, yes. And no. You have people who does make their own bad luck by doing stupid, risky things all the time. You have people who does like to surround theyself with people who so. That is a kind of bad luck that they bring on theyself, and so is not really bad luck, more bad judgement.

"But it have things that have such a bad history that they does carry a weight. You could call that bad luck. Like if a man kill another man without good reason, that man, you could say, go be bad lucky because he have the weight of that next man on he conscience. Or a thing, like a jewel, that a man thief from a sacred place and he had no right to touch, that could be a bad lucky thing."

Sonny fondled the ring in his pocket and thought some more. Glen Easton may have had something to say about back luck and the blood red ruby. So may have his brother.

"What if you don't believe in that?"

"You don't have to believe in air to breathe it," Papa Phil replied.

CHAPTER NINETEEN

Sonny and Clarence sat together on a boulder at the top of Rose Hill. It was nearly dawn. They had walked up there on Papa Phil's suggestion. "I know you don't believe in mourning ground," the Shango preacher said, "but it good to go off by yourself away from the world for a day to think about things. You mightn't get visions and catch power but it good to clear your head."

Clarence had come for the walk; he followed Sonny around all the time now.

"How much years you have, boy?" Sonny asked the child. It had been a week since they had met and there was still much he didn't know about the boy and his mother, even though he had nearly caused the death of one and had been to bed with the other.

"Nine. I go be ten in June," Clarence said. "Mammy promise me a present if I behave a good boy. I hope is not clothes," he said, screwing up his face. "Although I fed up wearing clothes from the boy living where she does wash for."

"You never went to school?"

"No. Mammy say she can't pay for books," Clarence said. Sonny knew poor boys all over the island faced the same fate. Those who could go to school usually stopped at age twelve anyway, before they could learn much more than their "three Rs": reading, writing and 'rithmetic. A boy like that could learn a trade, become a laborer, or do like the stammering boy and become a thug in the underworld. If that was to be Clarence's fate there was nothing Sonny could do to stop it.

"What you want to do when you get big?"

"I don't know," Clarence said. "I wish I could live somewhere like here, though. Somewhere with plenty trees. I never live nowhere like that before. Me and Mammy always live in town." He turned to Sonny with his own question. "You went to school?"

Sonny nodded. "Just for a little while when I was small. I mostly stay home and learn to read and write from my father and my grandmother. And I learn how to run a estate. That is a big place where they does grow trees and thing."

"Why you not doing that now? How come you is a police?"

Sonny smiled. "That is a long story. I like the estate but I wanted to see what else it had in the world. And I like to find out things. I did feel that if I was a police I could find out plenty things."

"That is true? Mammy say police just bad and don't care about black people."

Sonny laughed outright. "Some of them, yes. But I not so." But when he reflected on the work he was sometimes called upon to do—evict poor families for non-payment of rent on hovels too filthy for human habitation, break up church meetings, roust adult men and women for drinking liquor the State said was illegal because they couldn't tax it— he wasn't so sure.

In the east a glow began to appear in the sky. As he and the boy watched the golden yellow sun spilled into view. The clouds surrounding it turned pink, orange and then gradually white as within a matter of minutes the wonder of the sunrise gave way to prosaic morning.

The view at their feet was spectacular. A wide plain miles and miles long spread out to the south, jewel green and misty in the morning light. It was sugar cane, the economic giant in the island for the time being. Down in those fields of green, people would be starting their day's work.

Clarence set off down the hill and left Sonny on his own.

He had nothing but a calabash gourd of water. He started walking through the razor grass, along a path that resolved after some feet into a distinct track. At the end of the way there was a clearing. Mourning ground. Here Shango initiates spent a couple of days to a week fasting and praying, bathing in herbs and waiting for the coming of their spiritual guides. Pools of hardened candle wax of different colors showed where others before him had placed their faith in the universe. A universe of whose intentions Sonny wasn't clear.

He lay on his back in the warming sun, staring into the green forest surrounding the clearing. A bird twittered. Somewhere very far away a dog howled. Sonny closed his eyes and thought about his life.

When he came down the hill he was the same man he had always been. No visions, no epiphanies. But he knew what he had to do.

McLeod was pleased to see him, as usual.

"Where the devil have you been, man! Did you hear the news? You don't have to worry about Perro anymore. Someone broke into his house and shot him to death.

"Really?" Sonny asked. "Huh. Life is funny sometimes. But I came on other business."

He reached into his pocket and pulled out his service number, the nickel-cast badge police officers wore on their shoulders as an epaulet.

"I'll bring the other things by within the week."

Sonny stood and thrust his hand at the other man. "You've been a great boss, Inspector. I have enjoyed working with you. And I know we'll meet again."

McLeod looked at the shiny metal badge on his desk. "I won't accept this. I refuse."

Sonny shrugged. "I won't back down."

At the door, he turned back for a moment. "I think you should know that at least one policeman was working for Perro." He gave it a second thought. "At least two. You might want to check out your man Evers for any signs of sudden prosperity within the last six months." Someone had to have given the Venezuelan gangster Sonny's address and led them to Clarence. Evers was the likely candidate, having had easy access to Sonny's statement.

McLeod didn't look happy. "I'll hold this for a month before I report it. I hope you change your mind."

Sonny smiled. He wouldn't change his mind. He left the inspector's office and gently closed the door behind him.

Marie and Glass were all smiles when Sonny showed up at their cottage.

"We got the letter from Peters! Oh, Sonny!" gushed Marie, eyes glistening. "You're too generous."

"Hush up before I change my mind," he grumbled.

"Sonny, man, I don't know what to say," mumbled Glass, whose eyes were also suspiciously moist.

"Say thanks and nothing after that," Sonny advised.

"Thanks," the couple said in unison.

"So, what is this I hear about a baby?" Sonny asked his old friends.

Marie blushed. "How did you guess?"

"A birdie tell me. When it coming?"

"In about seven months. We're hoping for a girl this time," Glass said proudly. "Although if she's anything like her mother we go be in big trouble…"

Marie jabbed him in the waist and they laughed. It gave Sonny a stab of jealousy to see their rapport. Even at their best he and Joan had never been so comfortable with each other. But then they had only been talking to each other for a year before their two-month marriage and her disappearing act.

Marie seemed to notice his sadness. "When are you going to forget that foolish girl and settle down with a good woman? One who loves you as much as you love her?"

Sonny considered the question. He may have met a candidate for the position but refrained from comment. Instead, he said, "Glass, it have one more thing I want you to do for me."

His request brought a broad smile to Marie's face.

Mrs. Leila Ambrose was a dark-haired matron who hid her ageing complexion beneath a thick layer of pale makeup. Her glossy black hair was shot with streaks of red and Sonny guessed she dyed it with henna to cover her grey. She was English, judging by her accent. She was perhaps forty but looked older in spite of her efforts to the contrary.

Sonny got in to see her by writing a note. He didn't mince words. "I have the ring," the note said. She came down at once.

The parlor of the Gray Street mansion where she lived was as overdone as he would have guessed from the building's exterior. The walls were painted dark brown, with gold leaf on the grapevine molding that ran around the ceiling. A crystal chandelier illuminated the heavy, dark wooden furniture that dominated the floor. On the wall hung two paintings facing each other, a flattering oil portrait of Mrs. Ambrose and one of a portly, grey-haired white man with a handlebar moustache.

Sonny sat on one of the chairs. His hostess sat on one as far away from him as the room allowed.

"You have it," she said.

"Yes."

"Give it to me."

"No."

Her face reddened. Sonny would have bet money that she had never been spoken to in that tone by a black person before.

"Give it to me before I call the police."

"Mrs. Ambrose, I am the police." It was a little lie, but under the circumstances he felt it was justified.

"What do you want?"

"I want to see her."

"Never."

"If you don't send for her, I'll take this to Harding. I'm sure he'd be interested to find out how you've been aiding and abetting his wife in this affair." He took a chance that Leila had managed to keep the governor from knowing that.

From red she went nearly purple. Sonny began to fear for her health.

She picked up a bell and rang it. A uniformed maid came trotting in. "Tell Alfred to come. Now."

"Yes, M'um." The maid ran out.

"Will you excuse me, Mr....?"

"Yes." Sonny didn't feel obliged to give her his name at all.

She slipped out of the room and returned in a couple of minutes with an envelope in hand. Alfred, an old black man in a grey shirt and short pants, crisply presented himself. "Yes, M'um?"

"Take this to Lady Albertina. Tell her she is to come at once. At once."

"Yes, M'um." In moments Sonny heard a noisy car engine start up and drive off.

Mrs. Ambrose smiled tightly at him and said nothing more. Sonny settled into the wingback chair.

They didn't have long to wait. The car came back in less than half an hour.

Lady Albertina Harding breezed in. "I came instantly! What do you mean you found it! I thought it was lost forever! That's what Anto—" She spotted Sonny; the words dried up. "You!" she sputtered.

CHAPTER TWENTY

Sonny Stone wasn't a man easily forgotten. Lady Albertina Harding had spotted him through the window of the Ambrose house a few days ago. That was before he knew that he should have been looking for her all along. Miss Tina, as she apparently liked to be called, was at the heart of the murder of Glen Easton.

Sonny would probably never forget the look of the dead man facedown in the Dry River. Lady Albertina had never seen her lover dead after she had ordered his own brother to kill him.

She sat in the chair closest to him. Sonny could see her hands in her lap. They were lily white.

She flicked her short blonde hair out of her face with one of those white hands. "Who are you?"

Sonny could appreciate a man like Glen Easton falling for her charms. The governor's wife was a classical English beauty, with rose-pink lips, an aquiline nose and deep blue eyes. Unlike Mrs. Ambrose, she wore little makeup. If Sonny didn't know how filthy her heart was, he might have thought she looked like one of the pink and gold cherubs in his grandmother's illuminated Bible.

"I'm nobody. Let's leave it that way." He tugged the ring from his pocket. The heavy weight of the gold and the large ruby left a ghostly imprint in his hand after he tossed it to the blonde. "That's yours."

He was on his feet and nearly out the door before she got up to follow him, lightly resting one of her pale hands on his hard shoulder. "Is there something I can give you in return?" There was more than a hint of invitation in her crisp English voice.

Sonny shook off the hand. "Just forget about me. You have what you wanted. It's over."

She looked down at the ring, rich and blood red in the dim light of the room. By the time she looked up, Sonny was gone.

He took Vero back to his Duke Street apartment that evening, leaving her son with Papa Phil. As the sun was going down over the hills to the west of the city, he showed her what he could do when he wasn't sleeping on a wooden floor.

Afterwards, as they lay in bed, he asked her what she wanted to do with the rest of her life.

"Wash clothes." She shrugged. Her life wasn't as complicated as his. If she ever used to dream it had been beaten out of her by her first man, Clarence's father, ten years before.

Sonny told her he wanted her to consider sending her son to school.

"I can't pay for that," she said flatly.

Sonny cut in. "I go pay for it."

"Hmmm! Mr. Big Shot! I didn't know police used to make so much of money!"

"I quit. I ain't a police again."

She laughed outright. "So, you ain't working nowhere at all and you want to pay to send the boy to school?"

"I have some money put away," Sonny said lightly. "And I

ain't have no family. Well, I have a grandmother but she ain't need it. I must introduce you to her one of these days," Sonny said, idly tracing a pattern on her bare, flat belly.

"But before that, I have a friend I want you to meet again."

Her delighted laughter proved it was a re-introduction she enjoyed.

The next morning, a tap on the front door awakened him. It was Glass, holding a package wrapped in brown paper. Sonny greeted him in the doorway but didn't invite him in. Glass, seeing Vero's long, brown legs in the bed behind his friend, raised an eyebrow and said nothing, staying on the step. He handed him the package. Sonny tore it open eagerly.

"That is what you wanted?" Glass asked, critically eyeing the pane of etched glass.

"Perfect thing, man."

Sonny held it up. It read:

"Johnson Stone, Jr, Private Detective."

ACKNOWLEDGEMENTS

The character Sonny Stone is a fiction based on my research into the early 20th century histories of the T&T Police Service, the turn-of-the-20th-century cocoa bust, and the colonial city of Port of Spain. I set Sonny's story in Port of Spain in 1934 because my late mother lived there as a child around that time. I imagine Sonny walking the city streets that my mother could have walked, riding the tram, going to concerts in the Governor's bandstand, drinking fresh cow's milk from the colonial city's pastures as Dolsie might have done. Port of Spain is my home and my favorite city. This book is a love song to it and to my mother.

Death in the Dry River pays homage to the Yard. Historically, the Yard was a place of possibility, a basin into which human life spilled over from the houses and hovels and holes where the city's poor and Black resided, a place where they could claim their full humanity, where they loved, warred, made art and music, fed one another and kept African Trinidadian culture alive. Sometimes barracks rooms surrounded the yards, low-cost, cheerless and cramped quarters rented to the working poor in the inner city. Sometimes the Yard was found behind a striving single-family home in the city's suburbs, in places like Belmont, Newtown and Woodbrook. Other Yards were spiritual homes and community centres, like the All Stars and Renegades panyards in Port of Spain. They provided and continue to provide the city with heart and teeth and memory.

Death in the Dry River is a crime story. The villain of the piece is based on the real-life Trinidadian gangster Boysie Singh, and the victim is based on my research into the history of calypso and calypsonians at that time. Sonny's story is about a racially divided society in which the privileged pull the strings but not the triggers. It is regrettable that so little has changed in nearly 100 years.

To research and write a book is a shot in the dark when one is an unsigned and unpublished writer, which I was in 2005 when I wrote this novella. I fell in love with this world and its people and imagined I'd write a series, like the Easy Rawlins books by Walter Mosely, spinning the stories of my city's history into the kind of crime stories I'd like to read myself. Alas, this manuscript didn't sell until 2021, and just in time because the COVID pandemic cut me off from earning a living in Trinidad and Tobago. I especially thank my publishers, my dear friend keifel agostini and his wife Victoria Raschke, for supporting me again and again. I'm honored to join the stable of indie crime writers at 1000Volt Press.

I'm deeply indebted to Ishara, Judy, Gillian, Attillah, Jonathan, Verne, Brian, Harriet and Gareth, *Death in the Dry River*'s first readers. Thanks for the helpful comments and encouragement. I'm thankful to my proof-reader elisha bartels whose eagle eye rules over the Trinidad Creole used in the book.

Kim Johnson and the late Jerry Besson helped guide my research, for which I am thankful. Jerry passed before he could see this published but I hope he would have enjoyed it.

The staff of the University of the West Indies West Indiana and Special Collections Library at Alma Jordan Library, St Augustine, and the NALIS Port-of-Spain Public Library, especially the Heritage Library, helped me to find what I was looking for. I am thankful for them.

I am grateful to my family and friends for their continued support.

Finally, I bless God for His gifts.

Petit Valley, Trinidad & Tobago

October 9, 2023.

I delved into many sources to enrich my account of the life and times of Sonny Stone. I am grateful to the authors of the following:

James Cummings' *Barrack-Yard Dwellers*; Olga Mavorgordato's *Voices in the Street; In Celebration of 150 Years of the Indian Contribution to Trinidad & Tobago*; Ralph de Boissiere's *Crown Jewel*; CLR James' *Minty Alley*; Eustace Bernard's *Against the Odds;* Derek Bickerton's *The Murders of Boysie Singh*; Adrian Curtis Bird's *Trinidad Sweet*; Michael Anthony's *First in Trinidad*; Franklin's *The Trinidad & Tobago Year Book, 1932*; Bridget Brereton's *A History of Modern Trinidad, 1783-1962*; Debra B Whiteman's *The Immigration of Peons to Trinidad and their Contribution to the Development of the Cocoa Industry, 1811-1891*; and ER Moll's *Cacao in Trinidad & Tobago*.

Any errors in *Death in the Dry River* are my own.

Other Books Available from 1000Volt Press

The *Voices of the Dead* series and
companion cookbook
Verona Green
Victoria Raschke

Changing Paths
Yvonne Aburrow

Conjuring the Commonplace
Laine Fuller and Cory Thomas Hutcheson

Printed in Great Britain
by Amazon